BOOKS IN THE VAMPIRE DIARIES SERIES

CREATED BY
#1 *NEW YORK TIMES*
BESTSELLING AUTHOR

L. J. Smith

WRITTEN BY AUBREY CLARK

The Vampire Diaries

THE SALVATION

VOL. 1

UNSEEN

47N⬤RTH

Text copyright © 2013 by Alloy Entertainment and L.J. Smith
All rights reserved.

alloy**entertainment**

Produced by Alloy Entertainment
1700 Broadway
New York, NY 10019
www.alloyentertainment.com

Library of Congress Cataloging-in-Publication Data is available.

Published by 47North
P.O. Box 400818
Las Vegas, NV 89140

ISBN 10: 1477809678
ISBN 13: 9781477809679

Cover Design by Liz Dresner

A Note About the Hashtags in This Book

Elena's diary may be private, but this book doesn't have to be.
Everyone's talking about the biggest shockers, twists, and swoon-worthy moments.

Look for the hashtags throughout this book and share your own reactions on Twitter. To connect with other readers right now, tag your tweets with #TVD11.

ear Damon,

Yesterday, I felt happy. Not my usual everyday glow, but a wild, fierce happiness that ran along my veins like fire.

I would have known, even without the slight tug of the bond between us, that it came from you. It felt like you. What were you doing? Where were you yesterday?

I'm glad you're happy, Damon.

I miss you. Thanks to the bond the Guardians forged, we're never really far away from each other. I'm constantly aware of you, with a low-level hum of Damon-ness running through me. But I'd like to see you in person.

I can't believe it's been four years. I think of how we said good-bye, that last evening at Dalcrest, the bond between our auras so new, and how I cried, and I keep wishing I could have convinced you to stay.

Stefan misses you, too. We keep saying that soon, we'll take a few weeks and come find you, wherever you happen to be. Stefan can show me around streets he hasn't walked for centuries, and you can take us to the hottest nightclubs, and we'll all be together again. Family.

Sometimes I feel like I'm losing so much of my past. Aunt Judith told me yesterday that she wants to sell our house in Fell's Church and move to Richmond. It makes sense: Robert won't have so far to commute, and my little sister can go to a terrific school in the city. And after all, I don't live there anymore.

But I can't help remembering how my mother and I redecorated my bedroom there before she died, how many nights Bonnie and Meredith and Caroline and I spent there, having sleepovers and telling secrets. How you and Stefan each held me in your arms there, at different times and for different reasons.

I can say good-bye to that house, even though it hurts, but I can't say good-bye to you, too. Please, Damon, promise me we'll see each other again.

Elena Gilbert groaned and ran her fingers through her long blond hair. Why was it so hard to get to the point? She was getting distracted by her emotions, when she had meant to e-mail Damon for a reason.

But you already know I miss you, she typed.
Now there's something I have to warn you about.

Elena looked up from the laptop, glancing around her living room. Everything in her and Stefan's apartment was serene. Warm, golden lamplight illuminated the pale walls lined with framed reproductions from art exhibits she and Stefan had attended: an abstract of a couple embracing, their bodies melting into each other; a stern-faced Renaissance angel; a field full of wildflowers. Elena's little sister, Margaret, grinned up from her elementary school graduation picture on a table by the couch; in another photo, Bonnie and Elena stood in silver bridesmaids' gowns on either side of Meredith, whose face was lit up in a rare smile. Heavy brocaded curtains covered the windows, shutting out the darkness. Sammy, their long-furred white cat, stretched out luxuriously across the couch cushions, only a sliver of one golden eye showing he was awake.

On the top of a heavy mahogany cabinet rested the small collection of things Stefan had carried with him through all his years of roaming the world: a few gold coins, an ivory-hilted dagger, a stone cup mounted in silver, a gold pendant watch, and a small iron coffer. And finally, the most recent addition to his treasures: a silky apricot-colored hair ribbon, stained with mud, which Elena had once lost in a graveyard.

Elena remembered when she'd first seen these objects in Stefan's rooms in Fell's Church, back when he had been a mysterious, almost frightening, stranger. Now she knew the story behind each of them, understood all these talismans of Stefan's past.

The quiet apartment was practically the exact opposite of wherever Damon was right now, which was probably full of bright lights and fast cars. Elena had been so restless for so long—but, here, in the home she and Stefan had made together, she was content.

Of course, they were never completely safe. But since Klaus's defeat five years before, nothing more dangerous than a rogue young werewolf or newly made vampire had been drawn to the ley lines that crossed the Dalcrest area. They'd had to go farther afield to fight true evil; here they felt protected.

And she was happy. Mostly.

There was just . . . a persistent sense of danger that had been creeping up on her lately, invading her dreams with shadows, tugging insistently at the corners of her mind. And in the middle of this danger, she repeatedly sensed Damon's dark, fiery presence.

Frowning, she began to type again.

> *Wherever you are now, Damon, please be careful. I just know that something is wrong. I've tried and tried to find out what it is—stretched my Guardian Powers to their limit and even called Andrés in Costa Rica to see if he knew a way to pinpoint what I'm sensing—but I can't figure it out.*
>
> *All I know is that something awful is going to happen. And, somehow, you're involved. Please, Damon, be careful. I need you to be safe.*

Elena hit "send" on the e-mail just as a key rattled in the lock. Sammy leaped from the couch in one smooth flow of movement. Elena jumped up, too, and hurried toward the door.

"Stefan!" she exclaimed, pulling it open. "Welcome home!"

Even though Stefan felt as familiar and as essential as breathing by now, sometimes the sight of him still knocked Elena back a step. He was just so beautiful, with his classical Roman profile, his dark curls that made her want to tangle her fingers in them. His bottom lip dipped into a sensual curve as he smiled at her, his face opening in a way only Elena ever got to see, and she ran forward to kiss him.

She threw all her love into the kiss and felt Stefan's love in response, warm and reassuring.

Sammy twined around their ankles, sniffing Stefan, and then stalked away, his tail waving.

Finally Elena pulled back to look Stefan over and saw that, despite the dark shadows under his leaf-green eyes, his face was serene. The hunt had gone well, then. He was safe; Meredith was safe. Elena sighed gratefully and laid her head against Stefan's shoulder. He was home, and everything would be okay.

His arms tightened around her. The leather of his jacket was smooth under her cheek. Then she felt something sticky against her face. "Stefan?" she asked, pulling back and touching the wet spot on his black leather jacket. Her fingers came away red with blood. "*Stefan?*" she asked again, her voice rising, and began to feel frantically over his chest and sides, looking for injuries.

"Elena, it's okay." Stefan took her hands. "It's not my blood." His smile widened. "We killed Celine."

Elena sucked in a breath of surprise. They'd been hunting Celine for months. She was an Old One, one of the Original vampires—an ancient, vicious monster who'd stalked the night of every continent for countless centuries. Celine was the last of the three Old Ones they'd been able to find traces of, the last they'd needed to kill to make this part of the world safe.

At first, Elena had tracked her with Stefan and
Meredith . . .

* * *

*"Watch your head," Stefan told Elena, holding back a trailing
vine for her to duck under. Behind it was an ominous, dark opening, the entrance to a hidden cave. Meredith followed them inside,
her stave held at shoulder level in one hand, ready to strike.
Stefan's stave dangled more carelessly, held loosely in his grip.*

*"Celine's here; I'm sure of it," Elena said. She could feel the
Old One's presence, could see the trail of Celine's aura, peacock
blue twisted with gold and black, tarnished with the sickening
rust red of old blood. "She's really powerful," Elena whispered.
"And she knows we're coming."*

*"Terrific," Meredith muttered. They carefully felt their way
down the tunnel, half-blind in the darkness, Stefan leading the way.
The ground was rocky and uneven underfoot. Elena pressed her
hands against the cold stone walls to keep from falling. The tunnel
led deeper and deeper underground, and Elena breathed slowly,
trying not to think about the tons of earth and stone above her.*

*"It's okay," Stefan murmured, squeezing her hand. "She
can't hurt you." Nothing supernatural could hurt Elena—a
benefit of her Guardian Powers, and one they had to keep secret.*

*On the silver spikes at the ends of each stave was a telltale
darkness—tiny amounts of Elena's own blood, poison to any
Old One. Only her blood would kill Celine; only she could track*

Celine's aura. And she could feel her other Guardian Powers readying for the fight, gathering like thunderclouds.

Elena was ready. She wasn't afraid, she told herself fiercely. Stefan was right. Nothing supernatural could kill her.

They stepped cautiously around a curve in the tunnel and blinked, dazzled by a sudden flood of light. The sun shone through an opening somewhere high overhead, hitting the crystals that studded the cavern's walls, sending brilliant shafts of light everywhere. It took Elena a moment to realize there was a figure in the middle of the room, a pillar of darkness in the light.

The vampire stood as still and upright as a statue, her thick dark hair hanging heavy and long around her shoulders. Her aura swirled around her, tracing gold and rust red across her features, as though she were dripping with blood. She looked young, her face smooth and serene—until she raised her eyes to meet Elena's.

Her eyes were dark, empty—and old, very old. These were eyes that had seen civilizations rise from tiny villages to great cities and then fall into ashes, over and over again. Celine's delicate eyebrows arched, expectant and amused, as she gazed at them.

Elena stayed still in the entrance while Stefan and Meredith fanned out, heading in opposite directions along the side of the cavern, their staves poised, watching for their chance. Celine was too powerful for them to attack head-on, but if she were distracted, or if Elena used her Guardian Power against her . . . Meredith caught Elena's eye, and Elena reached for her

Power, understanding. Could she hold the Old One still long enough for one of the others to strike?

Celine stayed motionless, those cruel dark eyes fixed only on Elena. She can't hurt me, *Elena reminded herself. She took a deep breath and managed to snag the right trigger for her Power, like pulling a string. The energy gathering in her mind began to coalesce. She centered it, feeling the Power as solid as an arrow, directing it at Celine.*

The Old One's lips quirked into a smile. "I don't think so, little Guardian," she said, her voice rich with laughter. "I know your secret."

She raised one hand and made a quick plucking gesture at the ceiling. A heavy crack rang out through the air as the stone ceiling above them began to split.

"Elena, run!*" Stefan shouted. Before she could move, the rocks began plummeting down.*

"Stefan . . ." she managed to say, just as everything went black.

* * *

Elena winced, remembering how she'd woken up with a bad concussion, Celine long gone. After that, Stefan and Meredith had refused to let her come on the hunts. Since Celine somehow knew Elena could be killed by natural means—like a rock slide—but not supernatural ones, they thought it was too dangerous to let her get anywhere near the Old One. Elena had wielded her Guardian Powers from a distance, just as Bonnie and Alaric had researched and used magic to try to track Celine.

But now Celine was dead.

Ignoring the bloodstains, Elena tugged Stefan to her and kissed him, tenderly at first and then more deeply. "You did it. You're wonderful," she murmured against his lips.

She felt his mouth twitch into a smile, and he pulled back, cupping her cheek in one hand as he looked into her eyes, his clear-eyed gaze so full of love that Elena felt light-headed. "We couldn't have done it without you," he said.

"Well, *yeah*," Elena joked, glancing down at the slim leather case at their feet, which held Stefan's stave, the tiny silver hypodermics at each end filled with her deadly blood.

"More than just that," Stefan said, shaking his head. "I couldn't have done any of this without you. Elena, everything I do is because of you." His eyes shone, and he ran his fingers softly over her cheek. "And you're safe. This is the end. Now that Celine is dead, there are no more Old Ones."

"Not that we know of," Elena said, twisting her lips ruefully. If there was one thing she had learned over the past few years, it was that it was never truly over.

"But we're safe for now." He kissed her again, his body solid against hers. Elena let herself fall into the kiss. Their minds intertwined, sending each other love and desire, and then she reluctantly pulled away.

"We need to leave for Bonnie's birthday party in a few minutes," she said firmly.

Stefan smiled and pressed a soft kiss to the top of her head before stepping back. "It's okay," he said. "We've got plenty of time."

He headed for the bathroom to wash up, his stride loose and relaxed.

Elena looked after him thoughtfully. It was true. Now that Elena had drunk from the Fountain of Eternal Youth and Life, she would be beside Stefan forever. They had all the time in the world.

She knew she should be content. But with every steady beat of her heart, she couldn't help returning to the apprehension in the back of her mind. Despite their shared immortality, despite Celine's death, Elena had a bad feeling that time was running out.

2

Today, Bonnie felt happy. She had woken up to Zander cooking her a delicious breakfast, and the sun shining in her honor, on what really felt like the first day of summer. And then her entire kindergarten class sang "Happy Birthday" and presented her with a giant card that included twenty-one little painted handprints and twenty-one names, from Astrid to Zachary, printed in little-kid wobbly letters that she, Bonnie, had personally taught them to make over the course of the year.

"It was the cutest thing ever," Bonnie said, gazing happily around at her assembled friends. "One of the moms even baked me cupcakes."

And now she got to sit on a velvet chaise longue in a lovely bar full of Christmas lights and pink cocktails and enjoy herself.

Meredith, elegant as ever in a classic black dress, handed Bonnie a bubbling glass of champagne as she sat down beside her. Meredith's husband of six months, Alaric, patted Bonnie's shoulder affectionately before turning to pull over a seat of his own.

"Your class sounds adorable," Meredith said. "But I think *the cutest thing ever* might be that you got Zander to come to a cocktail lounge called the Beauty Mark."

"Zander likes to make me happy," Bonnie said simply. She glanced over to where her boyfriend straddled a tiny ornate golden chair with a pink leopard-print seat. She watched as Zander tilted the chair onto two legs and flung his arms wide, saying something to his Packmate Jared. The chair creaked and wobbled alarmingly under his weight. Bonnie winced. "It's possible this isn't his natural setting, though," she admitted.

Werewolf guys always seemed too big and rowdy to be inside, as if they might accidentally break things. Werewolf *girls*, on the other hand . . . Zander's second in command, Shay, met Bonnie's gaze and raised her own glass in a silent toast. Shay didn't get to do girlie stuff much and looked like she was enjoying herself. Bonnie squinted a little, catching a glimmer from Shay's pale skin. Was she wearing *body glitter*?

"Thank God Shay started dating Jared, right?" Elena said, plopping down on Bonnie's other side and following her gaze. Stefan, standing beside them, inclined his head to Bonnie in what was almost a formal bow.

"Happy birthday, Bonnie," he said solemnly, handing her two packages. The larger one was wrapped in polka-dot paper and tied with a pink bow; the smaller was much heavier and wrapped in a dark silk that shimmered with subtle rainbows.

"The big one's from us," Elena said. "The other one's from Damon. He sent it to us to give to you."

"Ooh, thank you," Bonnie said, looking at the packages with interest. She'd never gotten a gift from Damon before, but she had a feeling it would be something special. Damon was so elegant, so sophisticated, so intriguing, with his sleek dark hair and sharp smile that every so often softened for Bonnie . . . he was unlikely to give a girl, say, a DVD. Not that there was anything wrong with a DVD.

She politely opened Elena and Stefan's present first: a delicate filmy top she'd had her eye on when she'd gone shopping with Elena a couple of weeks earlier. "Gorgeous," she said with a wink, holding it up to herself amid a chorus of approval. "Thank you so much." She held out her wrist to Elena and Meredith, showing them a bracelet of gold filigree dotted with semiprecious stones. "Look at what Zander gave me! *And* he got me about a year's supply of dittany of Crete—an herb, for charm making," she added, for Elena's benefit. "It's really hard to find. He must have had to order it especially for me."

"It's beautiful," Elena said, and Meredith nodded approvingly. For such a *guy's* guy, Bonnie reflected, Zander was surprisingly good at buying presents for a girl. At least if that girl was Bonnie.

She couldn't concentrate on Zander's many wonderful qualities just now, though, not with a mysterious package from Damon in her lap, waiting to be opened.

She carefully unwrapped the silk. Inside was a small, rounded box that fit perfectly in the palm of her hand. It looked almost like a river rock, polished gray with a slight blue sheen to it. Opening the box, she found inside a delicate carved bird, in the same bluish-gray material, on a thin silver chain. There was also a note on thick, creamy paper, folded small.

"Wow," Elena said, bending to peer more closely at the bird. "What is it? It looks old."

Bonnie unfolded the note. In Damon's elegant script, she read:

> *My little redbird, congratulations on reaching the age of twenty-four. It's still ridiculously young, but at least you're not a child anymore. The enclosed comes from Egypt, and is older even than me. The bird is a falcon. A witch I met in Luxor tells me that it represents power, wisdom, and guardianship—all of which I wish for you. Be strong, be wise, be safe.*

Bonnie smiled. Damon could be surprisingly sweet and sentimental sometimes.

Underneath, in a different ink, scribbled in as if he'd added it at the last minute, was:

I hear you're still running around with the overgrown wolf boy. Tell him to behave himself or he'll answer to me.

Still sort of sweet, Bonnie decided, and tucked the note in her pocket.

"Here, let me fasten it." Zander came over and swept her hair aside, hooking the necklace firmly and then placing a swift kiss on the back of her neck.

"Damon called you an overgrown wolf boy," Bonnie told him. "You're supposed to behave yourself."

"Aw, he mentioned me?" Zander said affably. "I'm touched."

Jared snorted, and Shay's eyes narrowed. Most of Zander's Pack had never really understood Damon.

Or, Bonnie admitted to herself, they'd understood him too well. When the Pack had met Damon, he'd been going through a . . . difficult time. Truthfully, he'd been dangerous, and despite the fact that he'd fought beside them once or twice against greater threats, the small band of Original werewolves that protected the Dalcrest area didn't trust him.

But now that the Guardians had connected him and Elena, he wasn't so dangerous anymore. Because if Damon ever harmed a human, it would hurt Elena. If he killed anyone, Elena would die. And anyone who had seen Damon's fierce desperation when Elena was in danger knew he would never hurt her.

Besides, Bonnie thought pragmatically, the falcon weighing cool against her neck, it seemed like Damon was gone for good. Part of her missed him—there'd always been a special connection between her and Damon—but it might be better here without him. It was certainly calmer.

"Matt's here," Stefan said, glancing up from murmuring into Elena's ear. You could never surprise a vampire, Bonnie thought wryly.

But now they all saw Matt working his way over to their corner of the bar. He kissed Bonnie on the cheek and handed her a small package. "Hey," he said. "Happy birthday. Sorry I'm late."

"No problem," Bonnie said, surreptitiously feeling the present to see what it was. A DVD, she thought. "Where's Jasmine?"

Matt grimaced. "She really wanted to come, but she's on call for the emergency room," he said. "She said to tell you happy birthday and she'll take you out to lunch sometime next week instead."

"It's a pretty good excuse," Bonnie said. "You know, come to Bonnie's birthday drinks or be ready when they need you to save lives."

"Since Jasmine couldn't come," Matt said, smiling at Meredith and Stefan, "you can tell me what happened with Celine. She's dead?"

That was the one problem with Jasmine, Bonnie thought, taking a swig of her drink. She'd been dating Matt for a couple of years, and everyone really liked her, but she didn't know the truth about him, about all of them. Jasmine knew Bonnie liked fortune-telling, herbs, and "New Agey" stuff, but she didn't know she was really a *witch*. She knew Alaric had a doctorate in paranormal studies and folklore, but she didn't know any of *that* was real either; she just thought he was an academic. And she sure didn't know the truth about Stefan, or Zander and his friends, or Elena. She didn't even know Matt, not really, how he'd fought evil again and again, how strong and brave he was. She just thought he was a nice, ordinary guy.

Maybe Bonnie needed to slow down on the champagne cocktails, because she opened her mouth and heard herself say, loudly, "Matt. How can you love Jasmine, when she doesn't even know who you are?"

Matt's face stiffened, his mouth forming a tight line, and a hot flush of embarrassment ran over Bonnie. Wasn't she *ever* going to learn to keep her mouth shut? After a moment, Matt said stiffly, "It's safer for her this way." His light blue gaze met hers. "I just want Jasmine to have a normal life."

Bonnie's throat tightened. She remembered when she and Zander had finally told each other the truth about themselves, more than five years ago. How she'd held his hand, nervous. *Normal is overrated*, she'd told him, and they'd kissed, sweetly and honestly, everything open between them. She couldn't imagine keeping secrets from someone she loved for so long.

She managed to smile at Matt, although the smile felt pinched on her face, and nodded, blinking away the stinging in her eyes. "Okay," she said in a small voice.

There were an awkward few moments of silence.

"Anyway," Meredith said, with a brittle little laugh. "Since you asked . . ." She began to describe to Matt the battle she and Stefan had fought with Celine.

It was a dramatic story. There were secret passages and close calls and much use of Meredith's skills and Stefan's vampire speed and strength before they'd even gotten close to Celine. But finally they'd tracked her down in Atlanta, evaded her vampire soldiers, and killed her with Elena's magic blood.

The first two times they'd told the story tonight, Bonnie had been hanging on Meredith and Stefan's every word.

This time, though, she politely stifled a yawn and glanced around. Everyone else was still riveted. Even Alaric, who was usually Bonnie's compatriot in being more interested in the magical side of fighting monsters than the physical side, was asking intelligent questions about weaponry.

She sighed, dutifully fixing her eyes back on Meredith. It was possible, Bonnie admitted to herself, that she was a little bit jealous. They hadn't asked her for help at all in tracking down Celine.

Bonnie was good at fighting evil. It was just that, as her friends had become even more superpowered—faster, stronger, in Elena's case *immortal*—it was possible that they didn't really *need* her.

Bonnie pushed the feeling away and took another sip of her drink. *Stop being ridiculous*, she told herself firmly.

Meredith was reaching the end of her story—Stefan was about to cut Celine's head off, as the Old One writhed in her death spasms—when Zander caught Bonnie's eye and suddenly hopped to his feet, knocking his tiny gilt chair over with a clatter.

"Whoops," he said, winking at Bonnie as he sauntered closer. She grinned back at him. Maybe she hadn't been doing as good a job of hiding her emotions as she'd thought. "Time to toast the birthday girl," he announced, and everyone climbed to their feet.

"Okay," Zander said thoughtfully. "I'll go first. What is there to say about Bonnie McCullough that you don't all know already?" He pulled her closer, wrapping a warm, strong arm around her shoulder, and she leaned happily into him. "Well, there was the first night we moved into our apartment. It felt weird being in this brand-new place, and I couldn't sleep. But then Bonnie started telling me all about these myths she'd been reading about selkies. She was so smart and looked so gorgeous with the moonlight shining on her, that I would have fallen in love with her right then and there if I wasn't already fully and completely in love. And I thought, as I fell asleep, *Moving in with Bonnie is the best decision I ever made.*" He kissed her briefly, the corners of his sea-blue eyes crinkling affectionately, and raised his glass. "Which of course I already knew. To Bonnie!"

They all drank, and then Meredith cleared her throat. "I couldn't have gotten through the wedding without Bonnie," she said. Her olive cheeks flushed slightly as she added, "You all know what my parents are like. When I couldn't stand them taking over the wedding planning anymore, Bonnie and Elena would kidnap me and take me somewhere on a 'sanity outing.' The very best sanity outing was Bonnie's idea."

Elena started to laugh. "This was *completely* Bonnie's idea."

"They took me to the batting cages down at the park," Meredith went on, "and slapped a batting helmet on me and turned on the machine, and I whammed balls around until I didn't feel like running off to Vegas to elope anymore. And Bonnie sat there and shouted advice at me and bought me a hot dog when I was done." She slung an arm around Bonnie and hugged her tightly, pressing a cool cheek to hers. "Best friends ever."

"Me next," Elena said, as Meredith let go of Bonnie. "So, as you'll recall, Bonnie and Meredith and I spent all four years of college rooming together. When we graduated last summer, it was"—she shrugged—"scary. We weren't going to be there for each other every minute anymore. That last night, Bonnie decided we were going to have a slumber party just like the ones we had in junior high. We did one another's hair and nails and prank-called our boyfriends—"

"I was very surprised," Alaric added solemnly.

"It was a silly night," Elena said, "and it took Meredith and me a little while to get into the spirit of it, but Bonnie coaxed us along, and it ended up being perfect. Sisterhood." As Elena raised her glass, Bonnie suddenly remembered how Elena had looked that night, her usually perfect hair in a hundred sloppy braids, laughing in pink pajamas. Elena, she thought, needed to laugh more.

"Velociraptor sisterhood," she corrected, and Elena smiled at their old private joke.

Matt stepped forward a little. "My favorite memory of Bonnie this year is from Alaric and Meredith's wedding," he said. "Jasmine was still feeling awkward around you guys—she knew we'd been friends for a long time, and I guess it's weird for new people—"

"It *is*," Zander agreed loudly. "And Jasmine and I are both *awesome*."

Bonnie shushed him. "We're talking about me now, honey."

"Anyway," Matt went on. "At the reception, Bonnie took Jasmine under her wing, and before I knew it she was out dancing with all the girls and having a great time."

"Her dance moves put me to shame," Bonnie told him. Jasmine had looked gorgeous that night, her short teal dress setting off her long dark curls and caramel-colored skin. Most beautiful of all, though, had been the way her eyes shone every time she looked at Matt. Matt *deserved* someone who saw how great he was, Bonnie thought, and so she'd tried really hard to make Jasmine comfortable.

When Matt fell in love, he fell hard and for the long haul, and he hadn't had much luck in the past. Even if he wouldn't tell Jasmine the whole truth about himself, Bonnie wanted them to work out, for his sake.

Stefan raised his glass. "Bonnie, when I first met you, you seemed so sweet and innocent and *young*. I didn't take you as seriously as I should have. But it wasn't long before I came to realize how wrong that was. You are spontaneous and intuitive and have a warm, loving heart. Here's to your twenty-fourth year being even better than the last."

All Bonnie's friends were smiling at her, their glasses held up to toast, and she smiled back, warmed by the combined affection of their gazes. It was fine. Even if she wasn't *essential* to the monster fighting, she knew everyone loved her.

Today, Bonnie was happy.

3

"**Y**ou're being very boring, you know," Katherine called up to Damon from the piazza. "Come join us." Damon languidly waved at her from the balcony without looking up from the screen of his laptop. The sun had just set, but some light still lingered; dark shadows spread across the floor.

Something awful is going to happen, he read. *I need you to be safe.* He closed the laptop without replying to Elena's message and leaned back in his chair, frowning a little.

Then he felt for his connection with Elena—tentatively, as if he were lowering himself slowly into a deep, swirling river. The bond between them was always there, but Damon had gotten better at keeping it in the background, a mere comforting hum reminding him *Elena's there. Elena's there, and she's fine.*

But now he let his barriers fall. The sense of *ELENAELENAELENA* hit him like a tidal wave, and Damon went under for a minute, his senses flooded by Elena's emotions, Elena's essence. He could almost smell her: her pomegranate body wash, the faint coconut scent of her shampoo, and underneath it all the warm, tantalizing smell of Elena's rich blood. He caught a flash of quick images from her: the red of Bonnie's hair, something shiny glittering at the edge of Elena's vision. She was content right now, he realized, enjoying herself, and that told him all he needed to know. She was fine, and his brother, Stefan, was safe. Whatever new disaster was hovering at the edges of Elena's life, and of Damon's own, it had not yet arrived.

Maybe it never would. There would always be danger; Damon had accepted that centuries ago. And threats rarely came when you were expecting them. Even a Guardian like Elena could be wrong.

He stood up and stretched with a liquid grace, pushing his connection with Elena back to the edge of his consciousness. Sometimes, in the very early morning when he was settling to rest, Damon would open himself all the way to Elena just to feel her with him, the sense of her flooding through him as he lay back on his silken sheets. Usually she was sleeping then, deep in the dark of a Virginia night, and Damon could lose himself in Elena's dreams.

But touching Elena's mind like that always left a strange ache in Damon's chest afterward, so he tried to resist as long as he could. He didn't quite know what the sensation was. It couldn't be loneliness, because Damon was never lonely.

He wandered to the edge of the balcony and looked down into the piazza below. There were a few tables set around the grand fountain in the middle of the square, but only one was occupied. Katherine was not in the mood to mix with the locals, and so the locals had found themselves deciding to stay inside tonight.

Katherine looked up at him, her long golden hair falling over the back of her chair, and beckoned imperiously. Beside her, her current boyfriend, Roberto, glanced at Damon and then down at the table. "Come here," she said. "It's time for dinner."

Sometimes Damon couldn't believe he was still traveling with Katherine. He had never expected to see her again. But then, two years ago while wandering the streets of Tokyo, he'd caught sight of her through the crowd, felt the familiar brush of her mind, and she'd turned and smiled at him. He hadn't mistaken her for Elena—he never did, although they looked so much alike. And somehow, even after everything they'd been through, it had felt like the most natural thing in the world to cut through the crowd and take her hand. After all, he'd spent most of his long life loving her.

They'd been traveling together since then. And this much could be said for Katherine: She was infuriating at times, selfish and conceited, but she was never, ever dull.

More quickly than a human eye could have followed, Damon gracefully dropped from the balcony to the piazza below, his feet landing cat-soft on its cobblestones. Katherine smiled at him and patted the seat of the chair next to her.

"I'm starving," Roberto said sulkily, as Damon sat. "Where's the waitress?"

Roberto was always complaining, always on edge. Damon remembered what it was like to be a young vampire, restless and unable to settle, but surely he had never been as petulant as Katherine's latest toy. At least, Damon consoled himself, Roberto wouldn't be with them for long.

He wasn't the first handsome young man Katherine had picked up in their travels. There'd been Hiro in Tokyo and Sven in Stockholm, Nigel in London—Damon had actually liked Nigel, who'd at least had a sense of humor—and Jean-Paul in Paris. Roberto, with his dark hair and cleanly cut features, was just the latest. After a while, Katherine always left them behind.

But for now, she was still enjoying her new toy, and so Damon would tolerate him. Katherine patted Roberto on the arm soothingly. "Look," she said. "Here she comes." A pretty girl from the restaurant at one side of the piazza was hurrying toward their table, carrying a tray piled high with food and drink.

Damon smiled briefly at the girl as she placed a platter of figs and prosciutto before him. Picking up one of the ripe, firm fruits wrapped in salty meat, he bit into it and licked his lips. He didn't have to eat human food, of course, but sometimes he enjoyed the novelty of it.

"Bianca, come here," Katherine said to the waitress.

The waitress came and stood beside Katherine's chair, her face half-eager and half-shy. "*Si, signora?*" she said breathlessly, "You want—you want something from me?"

"Yes." Katherine stood and cupped the girl's face gently, gazing into her eyes. Damon felt a whisper of her Power. "You remember what I want," she said softly, soothingly. "It's all right with you. In fact, you'll enjoy it. Afterward, you won't remember anything about this until I tell you to. You'll just know that you want to do whatever makes us happy."

"Of course, yes." The girl nodded enthusiastically, her long chestnut hair falling across her face, brushing over Katherine's hand. "Whatever you want." She held out a hand to Roberto and he took it, cradling it against him as he bit deeply into her wrist and began to drink from the vein there.

Katherine turned Bianca's face toward Damon, both girls gazing at him with wide, untroubled eyes. "Do you want some?" Katherine asked. "I'm the one who's com-pelled her, so it won't violate your precious agreement with the Guardians."

Damon flinched involuntarily, then covered his reac-tion with a smile. Taking a sip from his bubbling glass of prosecco, he shook his head. "I don't want her," he said coolly, and watched, his face carefully blank and bored, as Katherine angled the girl's head and sank her fangs smoothly into Bianca's neck while Roberto continued to suck steadily at her wrist.

He could, technically, have drunk from the girl. Katherine was right: His deal with the Guardians was that *Damon* could not compel people to let him feed on them, not without hurting Elena. He could have spent eternity following Katherine, or any other vampire, around the world, feeding on humans they'd compelled for him, like a parasite. But the very notion disgusted him. He was Damon Salvatore, and he was no one's parasite.

Besides, he was doing just fine on his own.

Damon looked up to see Vittoria coming toward him, skirting around the fountain, where the dancing water reflected the lights of the piazza and made soft shadows across her skin. She was young, a university student, and still lived with her parents; she would have had to lie to them about where she was going. Her dark curls were knot-ted in a loose bun at the nape of her neck, and she held herself very straight, walking with the grace of a dancer. He got to his feet to meet her.

Vittoria glanced at Katherine and Roberto, drinking steadily from Bianca, then walked around them gingerly, averting her gaze. She stopped to stand before Damon.

"It doesn't hurt her," he said. "She'll be all right; she won't even remember."

"I know," Vittoria said solemnly, her eyes wide and disconcertingly trusting. Damon held out his hand, and Vittoria took it. Hand in hand, they crossed the piazza and sat on the edge of the fountain together.

"Are you sure about this?" Damon said, tracing the shape of Vittoria's fingers with his own. "I don't love you; you know that."

"I—I don't mind," Vittoria said, her cheeks flushing. "What you do to me. I like it," she added in a hushed, half-embarrassed voice.

"As long as you're sure," he told her, and she nodded, swallowing hard. Damon stroked a stray strand of hair back behind Vittoria's ear and pulled her closer. His sensitive canines extended and sharpened, and, as gently as he knew how, Damon slid them into the vein at the side of Vittoria's neck.

She stiffened in pain and then relaxed against him, her blood bursting into his mouth like the juice of a ripe plum. It wasn't as rich as Elena's, but it was sweet, filling Damon's mind with the images of young, soft-featured girls from his distant past, looking up at him with love and desire.

He remembered how nervous he'd been when he'd left Elena, how worried that, if he couldn't compel humans to let him feed, he would go hungry, or be reduced to stalking squirrels and foxes like his little brother. But it had turned out to be surprisingly easy.

He couldn't use his Power to compel human girls, but he could *charm* them. He could talk to them, flirt with them, smile into their eyes just as he had in Florence five hundred years ago, back when he was human and angling for nothing more than a kiss or two. It surprised him, how easily it came back to him. And he liked the girls he charmed, even loved each of them a little in his own way. Though he forgot them as soon as he and Katherine moved on.

It was very late by the time he'd finished and released Vittoria. She brushed a shy kiss against his lips and hurried away with a murmured good-bye, twisting a silk scarf around her neck to hide the mark of his bite.

Damon leaned back on his elbows and looked up at the stars. He felt someone sit down beside him, and shifted over to make room for Katherine.

"It's a nice night," she said, and Damon nodded.

"Clear, too." He pointed. "Polaris, the North Star," he said. "Leda, the Swan. They don't change, any more than we do."

Katherine laughed, a high, silvery sound like the ringing of a bell. "Oh, *we* change," she said. "Just look at us."

It was true, Damon thought, smiling despite himself at the challenge in her eyes. He'd known quite a few Katherines: the shy, clinging girl he'd met back home when he was human and she was newly made; the madwoman who'd pursued him to Fell's Church; and then this harder, brighter Katherine who had become, strangely, a friend. And he wasn't the angry young vampire who had woken on a cold stone slab beside his brother all those centuries ago, not anymore.

"Perhaps you're right," he admitted.

"Of course I'm right. Now, I'm thinking we should stay here for a while," Katherine said. "Roberto says the palazzo's owner wants to sell. We could settle in."

Damon sighed. "Everyone here knows who we are already," he said. "You feed on anyone who catches your fancy. It'll all end in pitchforks and torches, like a horror movie."

Katherine laughed again and patted his knee. "Nonsense," she said firmly. "They love us here. We haven't killed anyone at all, thanks to your newfound morals. To them, we're just the beautiful rich people in the palazzo who sleep all day."

Damon looked back up at the stars. Katherine was probably right; they were in no danger. He imagined staying here for a few years: eating figs, tossing coins in the fountain, drinking from sweet Vittoria and eventually her replacement.

But sooner or later, they would leave and continue their wanderings across the globe: Beijing next, maybe, or Sydney. He'd never been to Australia. He would charm another girl into loving him, taste the richness of her blood, be irritated by Katherine's latest toy, gaze up at the stars. They were all the same after a while, Damon thought, all the places of the world.

"It doesn't matter," he said finally, closing his eyes and reaching again for the faint thrum of *Elena* inside him. "Whatever you want."

4

"**B**onnie liked her present, don't you think?" Meredith asked, straightening the pillows on the couch. She cast her eye over the rest of the living room: her law books lined up neatly; the coffee table dusted and cleared of Alaric's research; the carpet vacuumed. She'd been gone for three days tracking Celine with Stefan, and she'd had some tidying to do when she returned. Alaric wasn't a slob, but he didn't keep things exactly the way Meredith did.

As she walked over to twitch the curtains straight, she caught Alaric's eye. He was leaning against the doorframe and looking amused, a mug in one hand.

"You knew I was compulsive when you married me," she said, and Alaric's face split into a grin.

"I did," he said, "and I married you anyway. But yeah, I think Bonnie loved the earrings." He crossed the room and laid his free hand on Meredith's arm, nudging her gently toward the couch. "Sit down and drink your tea. And then let's go to bed, it's late." She let him pull her onto the couch with him and leaned against him, nestling in Alaric's warmth. He smelled good, clean and soapy with an underlying Alaric-y whiff of spice.

"I'm glad to be home," she told him, and snuggled closer still. She was getting sleepy. "I'd better study some before I come to bed, though," she added dutifully. "Mock trial Monday. We're all really stressed out." The mock trials competition was a big deal, and she was the prosecuting attorney for her team.

Meredith adored law school. It was a culmination of all her love of logic and study, rules and case histories and solvable problems lining up in neat rows for her to master.

Kicking off her shoes, she curled her feet under her and sipped her tea, grimacing at the bitter, acidic taste of vervain. The mix of herbs Bonnie concocted for her friends was heavy on the vervain—which protected the drinker from being compelled—but the first taste was always unpleasant.

"More honey?" Alaric asked, but Meredith shook her head.

"I want to taste all of it," she said, and tried another sip, concentrating. The second time, it wasn't quite so bad. Underneath the bitterness of the vervain was the faint sweetness of lavender and a rich touch of cinnamon.

"I don't know why you won't just sweeten it up," Alaric said, shifting so that he could dig his thumbs into her vertebrae, kneading her shoulders with his fingers. "That's nasty stuff."

"I want to taste it all," Meredith repeated sleepily. It had been a long day, several long days, and she was ready to spoon up against Alaric in their wide, soft bed and go to sleep. *Work*, she reminded herself. *You're going to win this trial.*

Alaric worked a knot out of her shoulders, and Meredith moaned in pleasure. "You have no idea how tight my back got while we were gone," she told him.

"Oh, Stefan doesn't do this?" Alaric said teasingly. "Thank God, I was wondering what I had to offer that your hunting partner couldn't."

"Trust me, you've got lots to offer," Meredith said with a smile. Alaric brushed her hair aside and focused on the massage while she looked happily around the room. Her law books sat on the shelf, her slim silver computer on the desk next to a stack of Alaric's old manuscripts. Her hunting stave, in its case, was tucked in the corner. On the side table were various pictures of their friends, their wedding.

And a picture of Meredith, ten years younger, her arms around her twin brother, Cristian, both of them grinning. She didn't really remember Cristian—this reality where they'd grown up together was one the Guardians had created—and she didn't like to think about his death. Becoming a vampire was one of the worst fates she could imagine for a hunter.

Half-consciously, she leaned back against Alaric's hands, and he kneaded her muscles harder, comforting. Lately, she'd been coming to terms with the idea of Cristian. He'd grown up part of her family, in this life, and he mattered, whether Meredith remembered the young boy in the picture or not.

All the elements that made up her life—hunting, school, becoming a lawyer, her friends, her family, Alaric—they all mattered. She'd been so used to thinking of hunting as what defined her—that everything else was a gloss over her secret life, part of her disguise. That all she truly was, was a hunter.

But Meredith was going to be a *lawyer* now. She was somebody's *wife*. She was a friend and a daughter, and once she'd been a sister. These things were real to her, and they all mattered. Just like Bonnie's vervain tea, the bitter and sweet and spicy all mixing together, making up a whole.

"I want to taste it all," she murmured a third time, sleepily, and Alaric snorted with laughter.

"You're just about talking in your sleep," he said. "Time for bed. Everything will still be there in the morning."

He swung her up into his arms, and she buried her face in the crook of his neck, giggling sleepily, as he carried her to bed.

* * *

It was a beautiful night. Stefan opened his senses to everything around him, unusually eager to drink it all in. He could smell magnolia flowers in the yard of a house a few blocks away, the spices and grease of three different restaurants on the street he and Elena were walking up, the sour scent of beer coming from a bar halfway down the street, the warring perfumes of three girls getting out of a car near the curb. He could hear a hundred conversations, from the drunken argument of four frat boys in the bar to the loving whispers of a newly engaged couple in the Indian restaurant. In the apartment over a storefront farther down the block, a sad song played on a cheap radio.

The world had so much in it. He could feel the slow beat of his own heart, slower than a human's, and for once, its pace didn't feel like a reproach. For once, despite everything, despite what he was, Stefan felt *alive*.

So much to hear, to smell, to see, to feel. And most of all, Elena. Her hand was soft and strong in his, and she smiled at him, radiating love like a vibrant, glowing sun. His mind brushed against hers, and he could feel her welcoming him home, the familiarity and warmth of her.

He stopped suddenly in the middle of the sidewalk and kissed her. All the sensations and impressions that had been flooding through him narrowed down into one thing: Elena's lips, soft against his. Elena's warm breath. He sent her thoughts of *love*, and of *forever*, and she sent them back to him.

When they broke apart, they clung to each other for a moment breathlessly. Then Elena smiled and pushed her hair back behind her ears. "You're happy to be home," she said.

Stefan took her hands in his. "Now that Celine is dead, there can't be too many Old Ones left," he said. "When we find them, we can kill them, and then we'll be able to do anything we want, go anywhere we want."

Elena frowned, her eyes puzzled. "We can do anything we want *now*, Stefan," she said. "We don't have to wait and be sure all the Old Ones are dead. We can't wait for that."

Twining his fingers with Elena's, Stefan smiled down into her eyes. "Remember how, when you drank the water from the Fountain of Eternal Youth and Life, you told me you finally knew what our future would look like?" he asked. "I've always known—I've known for so long that *you* were my future, that you were the only thing I needed."

Elena's eyes shone. "I know," she said. "Stefan, I want that, too. I want forever." Then her mouth lifted into a mischievous grin. "But we've got forever, don't we?" She moved closer to him still, her soft hair brushing his cheek, her lips only millimeters from his, teasingly light. "I want to enjoy *right now*."

Stefan was lowering his head to meet her lips once more when someone suddenly lurched against them. Elena's breath puffed out in a soft huff of surprise, and she stumbled back a little, away from Stefan.

Immediately tense, Stefan felt himself fall into a fighting stance, his hands drawn up in fists. It took him a moment to realize there was nothing sinister here, no one he needed to defend Elena from. Just a group of people coming out of a bar, accidentally brushing against them. He shook off his aggression; he'd spent too long on the hunt lately.

"Sorry, sorry," one of the guys said, holding up his hands apologetically. He smiled at them. "My fault. Are you okay?"

The stranger was tall, taller than Stefan, with sharp cheekbones, longish sand-colored hair, and curiously yellowish-green eyes, glowing like a cat's, or a coyote's. He wasn't a vampire, though, Stefan sensed with a quick brush of Power—just another human out for an evening with his friends. Elena murmured that everything was fine, no harm done.

"It was our fault," Stefan said courteously, and moved aside. But the stranger didn't walk on right away. He was looking at Elena. Their eyes caught for a moment, Elena's face creasing into a tiny frown as her clear blue gaze met the stranger's yellowish-green one—and then the moment was over. Stefan shook off the strange feeling their locked gazes had given him. Elena was beautiful; he should be used to people looking at her. With another murmured apology, the stranger moved on down the street, his friends reforming into a group around him.

Elena turned her attention back to Stefan, putting her arms around his neck and pulling him back down for another kiss. "Where were we?" she said, laughing up at him. "Right here? Right now?"

5

"If your little pet is going to drag us all over the countryside, you're taking me out for a drink later," Damon told Katherine in an undertone, flashing a false, bright smile as he climbed the winding tower stairs.

"Oh, don't be a grouch, Damon," Katherine said sweetly. "You have to admit it's lovely here."

"I don't have to admit anything," Damon said, but he felt the edges of his mouth tugging up in a more honest smile.

For days, Roberto had been begging to explore the white medieval tower they could see from the windows of their palazzo, in the rolling green hills outside of town. Tonight, Katherine had finally agreed to take him, like an indulgent parent giving in to a petulant child. For lack of any better options, Damon had consented to come, too.

Roberto ran eagerly ahead of them; Damon could hear his feet clattering on the stairs above their heads. The top of the first stairway opened into a large square room with a worn wooden floor, empty except for a huge fireplace at one end, but by the time Damon and Katherine stepped inside, Roberto was already climbing the next set of stairs.

"*Avanti*!" He called back in Italian, urging them on.

"Modern Italian doesn't sound right to me." Damon sighed, a little wistfully. "Back in my homeland, and the children here speak garbled trash."

"Things change," Katherine said with a shrug. "Like we said last night, even we do. I was born in the Hapsburg Empire, and it doesn't even *exist* anymore. You and I, we just adapt and keep going." She slid him a sidelong look as they entered the next stairway, and her voice dripped with false sympathy. "Are you having a midlife crisis, Damon? Do you want me to hold your hand?"

Damon sneered halfheartedly at her. "As if I actually care about the decline of the Italian language," he said. "It's only that . . . this was home once, and now it's just another place." What was curious, and a little alarming, he admitted to himself, was that the thought of *home* now brought to mind a small town in Virginia and the faces of a bunch of American children. Principally, of course, a face much like the one laughing back at him as Katherine sprang ahead up the stairway.

At the top of the tower, the starlit countryside stretched out before them. The surrounding area was full of vineyards, and the smell of growing grapes and warm earth rose up all around. The sun had set more than an hour ago, but the air was clear, and Damon could see the lights of the town in the valley below them. The moon was full and large, hanging low in the sky—a harvest moon.

"It's so beautiful here. I love places like this." Roberto took Katherine's hand. "Was it like this, did you live somewhere like this, when you were alive?" His voice was full of longing, as if he was about to burst into an ode to Katherine and how he wished he could have known her always. Damon almost snorted when Katherine's eyes softened in response. It looked like Katherine was still finding little Roberto charming, which meant the boy would be traveling with them for a while longer.

Katherine was just beginning to answer when Damon stiffened and held up a hand to quiet her. There had been something . . . it came again. A small sound, the brush of a quick light step.

"Someone's coming up the stairs," he said.

Katherine cocked her head questioningly, and Roberto frowned, listening.

And then feet pounded on the stairs, all attempts at quietness abandoned. Alarmingly fast, before even Damon could move, a pack of people burst through the doorway and were upon them.

One caught Damon by the arm and threw him hard, so that he landed sprawling at the edge of the tower roof. He rolled quickly to his feet. *Not people, then.* Too fast, too strong. Something else.

The leader, a tall woman, bared her teeth, and Damon realized. *Vampires.* How had he not sensed them?

The tall vampire who'd led the charge held Katherine's arms pinned behind her and was angling to bite at her throat. Damon leaped toward them, throwing the attacker back while Katherine turned to quickly tear out her throat. A gout of blood sprayed across the white stone of the tower. Damon recovered quickly, back on the offensive, but there were too many of them, and they were already pressing closer, undeterred by the first vampire's death.

Instinctively, Damon and Katherine moved back to back, uniting against the threat, and Katherine pulled Roberto behind them, shielding the young vampire. Damon could feel her breath speeding up, and then she snarled, her hands bunching into claws. She was a good ally to have at his side.

There were so many of them, though, at least fifteen. Where had they come from, and what did they want?

Then several attacked Damon at once, snarling, coming from all three sides. The one in front of him, a dark-haired man, punched him in the face and moved back before he could respond, then punched and dodged again as the others worried him with teeth and nails from either direction. They were trying to get him away from Katherine and Roberto, Damon realized, trying to separate them so their opponents could use their greater numbers to overwhelm them.

Quick as a striking snake, Damon snapped the neck of one of the vampires attacking him from the side. He bared his teeth in a wild, joyous smile, then charged forward to grab hold of the dark-haired vampire in front of him, propelling him backward to the edge of the tower and sending him over in a flurry of flailing limbs. Not that the fall would kill him, but it would get him out of the picture, at least for now.

As Damon turned back from the edge of the tower, though, his heart sank. There were still far too many of them. And these weren't weak, newly made vampires either—they were strong and fast.

Katherine was holding her own, her face drawn into a snarl as she grappled with one of the attackers, ignoring another that was clawing ineffectively at her back.

But Roberto was in trouble, cornered on the far side of the tower.

Another vampire clutched at Damon before he could move toward the boy, and they tussled for a moment. His opponent swung him around, and Damon barely managed to dodge the stake a second vampire was aiming at his chest. Angry, he tore the stake from the second vampire's hand and stabbed it into the vampire's throat.

Shoving past them, he headed toward Roberto, who was struggling frantically, his face pale. The boy had probably never been in a fight before, not even when he was human, Damon thought in annoyance. But then Katherine screamed, and Damon turned to snap her attacker's neck.

"Katherine! Help!" A desperate gasp.

Katherine and Damon both looked toward the other side of the roof just in time to see Roberto's terrified face. A fierce-looking girl, younger even than Roberto when she was made, grabbed hold of his head as he fell and *pulled*. With a terrible ripping sound, Roberto's head was torn away from his body.

Katherine gave a strangled cry.

A few feet from them one of the wounded vampires struggled to her feet, her torn throat already healed.

"That's it; we're leaving," Damon said sharply. Taking a firm hold of Katherine's arm, he dragged her the few steps to the edge of the tower. Before any of the vampires following them could catch them, he leaped out into the darkness, taking Katherine with him.

They landed in a crackle of grape vines and the smell of dry earth. Catlike, Damon was on his feet in an instant. The vampire he'd thrown over earlier didn't seem to be anywhere around, he noted thankfully. He was probably already back up on top of the tower.

"What's going on?" Katherine asked, her voice harsh, her blue eyes narrowed with fury. "Why—who hates us? Who would want to kill us now? Klaus is dead. There's no one—"

"We don't have time for this," Damon said tightly, cutting her off. He could hear steps on the tower stairs. Their leap into the night had bought them a few minutes at best, and their attackers weren't going to give up so easily. "Come on," he said, taking Katherine's hand and pulling her roughly after him.

Damon and Katherine ran through the vineyards, plants crunching beneath their feet. They hadn't fed yet tonight and had used up too much Power in the fight to shift shape and fly, as Damon would have preferred. The most important thing was to get away.

At last, deep in the woods outside the little town where they'd been staying, they stopped to listen.

"I think we've lost them," Katherine said.

"For now." Damon frowned. "This wasn't a random attack. They must have been tracking us."

Katherine nodded. "Is there anything at the palazzo you can't stand to lose?" she asked.

Damon thought briefly of his favorite jacket, of a bracelet he had bought with the vague intention of sending it to Elena, of sweet Vittoria and her warm, fresh blood.

"Nothing that can't be replaced." Hesitantly, he touched Katherine's arm. "I am sorry about Roberto," he said.

Katherine's jaw tightened, and Damon thought he caught the shine of tears in her eyes, but her voice was level. "It happens," she said. "But he was awfully young. I would have liked to have taken him somewhere he'd never seen before."

Damon glanced up at the moon, which hung high in the sky overhead. It wasn't late yet; the trains would still be running. If they made it to the station, they could be across the border before dawn. "I think it's time we left Italy," Damon said softly.

6

Elena drove slowly down one of Dalcrest campus's side streets, looking for a parking place. There was an antiquarian bookstore around the corner, and she knew they had a collection of the medieval poetry Stefan liked. It would be nice to give him a little welcome-home present, she thought, smiling in anticipation.

Suddenly and without warning, her throat constricted and a bolt of panic shot through her. *Damon.* Somewhere, Damon was in trouble.

She involuntarily jerked the wheel aside and just managed to avoid sideswiping a parked car. His emotions ran through her, much stronger than usual, overwhelming her senses. Anger, and a sharp sense of fear, rage, a sort of adrenaline-fueled exhilaration. Was he fighting? What was going on? Panicked tears rose in her eyes—her own, she thought, not Damon's—and she blinked them back.

She needed to go home. She had to get to Stefan, let him know something was wrong. Taking a deep breath and trying to calm down, Elena took a sharp right and headed back toward the highway.

The road was clear ahead of her. Pushing Damon's emotions away, she risked fumbling in her purse for her phone. It was evening right now in Italy, where Damon had been the last time she had heard from him. But he could be anywhere, really. He traveled from country to country the way most people crossed streets.

Just as her hand closed around the phone, another flash of emotion from Damon broke through—fury, followed by a feeling of cold calculation. Whatever was happening to Damon, he was plotting a way to get through it. It made her feel a little better. If Damon was good at anything, it was surviving.

Elena quickly punched Damon's number into the phone, but it went straight to voice mail.

"It's me," she said to the electronic silence, the full distance between her and Damon stretching into infinity. "I felt something from you all of a sudden, something bad. Are you okay? Please call me."

As she ended the call, she pushed down hard on the gas pedal, the tires squealing as the car jumped forward.

Stefan would know what to do. Suddenly she was desperate to get home to him, to his comforting arms and his always-practical mind.

She pushed her foot down on the gas again, and this time, the pedal sank unresistingly to the floor of the car. Jerking, the car sped faster, much faster than Elena had expected.

Instinctively, she hit the brake, but nothing happened. Trees and telephone poles whipped past in a blur of green and brown.

Tightening her grip on the wheel until her hands ached, Elena slammed down on the brake again. The car didn't slow, but the wheel began to vibrate in her hands, small tremors at first, becoming faster and faster. Her heart raced, and a tiny panicked whine came from Elena's throat.

The car was beginning to drift across the highway, and another car swerved around her, honking loudly. She yanked on the wheel, trying to get back into her own lane, but it only spun uselessly under her hands.

"Come on, come on," Elena whimpered, pleading with the car, or the universe. "Please, no."

This is it, she thought with a blank feeling of wonder. After everything that had happened, after all she'd survived, she was going to die here, in an out-of-control car on a bright, sunny afternoon.

Something huge and dark rose up in front of her. *I'm sorry, Stefan*, she thought, and then everything went black.

* * *

"Elena? Elena?" A faint, unfamiliar voice was calling to her through the darkness. Elena twitched with irritation. She didn't want to talk to anyone; she wanted to sleep. Her head hurt and her chest ached terribly. Was she sick?

"*Elena!*" A pounding noise, somebody banging near her head.

With a huge effort, Elena managed to drag open her eyes. Everything was blurry and white, too close, and she pushed at the whiteness, trying to shove it away. It shifted under her hands with a rustling of fabric, and slowly the world came back into focus.

The white stuff was an air bag, she realized, and it filled the space in front of her. *I must have hit something*, Elena thought dazedly, and raised her hand to the pain in her head. Her fingers came away bright red, wet with blood. There was an aching, bruised feeling in her chest, and she scrabbled at her seat belt, smearing the blood across her shirt.

A wave of panic washed over her. She could have *died*.

"Elena!" the voice snapped at her again, and she jumped.

A guy a few years older than she was, with short dark hair and heavy brows, stood just outside her window, rattling her door handle. "Elena!" he said sharply. "Hurry! You have to get out of the car."

The intensity in his voice had Elena reaching automatically for the door handle, but then she drew back her hand. "Who are you?" she said warily through the glass. "How do you know my name?"

"There's no time to explain. Please just trust me. I'm on your side." His hazel eyes were steady, pleading with her. "You *have* to get out of the car."

Something in his voice made her hurry to unfasten her seat belt and open the car door. But before she could say anything, he locked onto her arm and dragged her down the side of the road, away from her car.

"What are you doing?" Elena exclaimed, trying to dig in her heels and pull away. "Let go of me!" It was broad daylight. "Help!" she screamed, her voice shrill in her own ears, but no help came. She glanced around wildly, but there were no other cars in sight. The guy's hand was like an iron band around her wrist, yanking her on.

She was drawing her breath in to scream for help again—surely there must be *someone* within earshot— when her captor came to a halt and let go of her.

"Okay," he said, resting his hands on his knees and taking in great gulps of air. "This ought to be far enough."

"What the hell do you think—" Elena began hotly.

And that was when her car exploded.

It went up in a great orange ball of flame and an ear-crunching boom, just like in the movies. A heavy cloud of oily black smoke rose from the flames.

Elena's body felt numb. Her stomach rolled with nausea as she blinked in shock at the dark smoke, the hungry flames.

She'd felt so safe as a Guardian. She didn't have to worry about getting old, or getting sick, or dying at the hands of vampires, or demons, or werewolves, or any other kind of *supernatural* being. All she'd had to worry about, Elena had thought, were very *human* causes of death—a knife, a gun, strangulation.

A car exploding in the street, with her inside.

Her mother had died in a car accident, even though she had been a Guardian, even though she'd been hundreds of years old at least, and Elena wondered why she had never really considered the same thing happening to her. She wrapped her arms around herself, unable to tear her gaze away from the burning car.

The dark-haired guy was standing next to her, watching the fire with a mildly intrigued expression, as if it were a TV show or science experiment. He was only about Elena's own height but had well-muscled arms and shoulders, like an athlete. "I'm Jack," he said, seeming to feel Elena's gaze on him. She automatically gathered her Power and used it to see his aura, which seemed warm and brown, sincere.

"That's not supposed to happen," she said, and flushed, because the words sounded stupid to her own ears. "I mean, I read an article about movie clichés, and a lot of it was about how cars almost never explode. Certainly not just from running into a tree." As she spoke, she felt her heart steady. If they could talk logically about the *why* and the *how*, maybe she wouldn't have to think about the *what*. The fact that she could have been gone forever, never see Stefan or Damon again.

"It was a telephone pole," Jack said drily, and then the corners of his mouth turned up in a sudden and unexpected smile. It changed his whole face. He looked friendly and open, and Elena knew her earlier instinct to trust him had been the right one.

She tried to take a step and stumbled, feeling suddenly sick. Jack hurried forward to steady her, concern etched on his face.

"We need to get you home," he said, his hand under her arm, supporting her. "And you're right. This doesn't just happen." They both turned to look back at the steadily burning car.

"I don't understand," she mumbled. She felt like she might laugh, or scream. Possibly she had a concussion, because nothing seemed to be making any sense.

Jack wiped his hand across his face in a quick, nervous gesture. "Elena," he said, "this was no accident."

7

"**I** should have been there to protect you," Stefan said wretchedly, wrapping his arms around Elena and burying his face in her hair. "I'm so sorry." While he had been relaxing in the apartment, Elena had almost *died*. And he wouldn't have even known until the police came to their door.

The world swung dizzyingly, and he clutched at her for balance. The thought of Elena dying was like an endless fall into a dark void. Elena had never been safe, never would be, no matter how many Old Ones he killed.

"There's nothing you could have done, Stefan," Elena said calmly, steadying him. She glanced around the room at all of her worried friends. Her eyes landed on the stranger—Jack—who had gotten her out of the car after the crash and brought her home. "It all happened so fast."

"Thank you for helping," Stefan said to Jack. Jack nodded pleasantly from his seat on the couch. He seemed to be taking everything in, his dark eyes flicking over the whole group with interest—maybe too much interest. He hadn't called the police, hadn't taken Elena to the hospital; he had just brought her home. Jack was an outsider; what did he think was going on?

"The important thing is to make sure that Damon's all right." Elena let go of Stefan and sat down beside Jack on the couch, closing her eyes with a little frown. Stefan knew she was reaching for her bond with his brother. He did his best to push down the jealousy that threatened to break the surface. Elena loved him; *he* was the one she'd chosen. But it was hard to accept the fact that she and Damon shared something that he couldn't really understand. "Whatever's going on, it doesn't feel like he's in danger now," Elena said after a moment.

Stefan breathed a sigh of relief, realizing belatedly that Jack must think they were crazy. But his gaze remained polite and attentive.

Meredith came back in from the kitchen with a washcloth, brushing past Bonnie and Matt, and sat down between Jack and Elena to dab carefully at the blood on Elena's forehead. "It looks like the cut's all healed up," she said. "And your pupils are normal, so you're probably not concussed anymore."

"Score one for the amazing properties of vampire blood," Elena said, smiling up at Stefan.

Stefan flinched backward, feeling his eyes widen. Meredith frowned in surprise, and Bonnie looked up from the floor by the couch where she was going through a bag of herbs, her mouth open in surprise. Matt had been worrying silently in the side armchair nearby, but now he unclenched his jaw to protest, "Elena . . ."

"It's okay," Elena said, tipping her head back to smile reassuringly up at Stefan. "Jack knows all about us. He was following me because he wants to talk to us."

A chill ran through Stefan—*all* about them?—and he felt his eyes narrow suspiciously. In a second, he was looming over Jack. Grabbing the front of his shirt, he yanked him to his feet. "You were *following* her?" he asked, his voice low and dangerous.

Jack held up his hands. "Wait," he told Stefan, "I'm on your side. I helped Elena."

"I have to ask," Meredith said dryly, folding the wash-cloth and dropping it on the coffee table. "If you weren't the one who tampered with Elena's car, how did you know it was going to blow up?"

Jack chuckled and leaned back, pulling his shirt out of Stefan's hands. "I like you," he told Meredith. "I bet your dad's really proud of you."

Before Meredith could snap a reply—after all, Stefan thought, it was a patronizing thing to say—Jack raised his hands and crooked his pinkie fingers together, balling his other fingers into fists and bringing his thumbs together above them to make a triangle.

The sign meant nothing to Stefan, but Meredith gasped. "You're a hunter," she said, in a far less confrontational voice. "You know my father?"

Jack smiled. "Not personally, no. He doesn't have contact with hunters anymore; I guess you know that. But 'Nando Sulez is a legend. It's an honor to meet his daughter."

The hard line of Meredith's mouth softened in surprise, and Stefan backed off a little, still suspicious. "The fact that you're a vampire hunter hardly gives me a reason to trust you," he said. Elena reached a hand out to touch his leg, her thumb running comfortingly across his calf.

"It's okay," she said softly. "I've looked at Jack's aura. He's good."

Sighing, Stefan thought about all the ways that someone could be a good person and still want to kill vampires. Still, he had to trust Elena: Her instincts about people had always been sound, even before her Guardian Powers were awakened. "You haven't answered the question," he said to Jack, keeping his voice polite. "How did you know the car was going to explode?"

"My team—there are quite a few of us in town now—we know how powerful Elena's blood is, that it's the only real threat to the Old Ones." Jack's eyes flicked around the group. "When we realized that Solomon was headed for Dalcrest, we assumed he was coming to eliminate Elena. And when I saw Elena's car crash, I felt sure that Solomon was involved. It seemed smartest for her to get away from the car."

"Wait a second. Who is Solomon?" Bonnie asked. Elena's white cat, Sammy, had stretched out on his back in her lap. Bonnie rubbed his belly without looking down at him, her fingers twining through his fur affectionately.

"Solomon's an Old One," Jack said heavily. "Maybe the last of the Old Ones."

Stefan's heart sank. Elena had been right; there was always danger. How naive of him to think that, just because they'd killed all the Old Ones they could track, there weren't others tracking *them*. And this one must know about Elena's secret weakness, if he had tried to kill her with a car accident. Elena was frowning worriedly, obviously having realized the same thing.

"I think I know a spell that'll help protect your next car," Bonnie said, her jaw stubbornly set. "I don't know how well it'll defend against deliberate attacks, though. I'll do some research."

Meredith took Elena's hand. "Hey, we've killed Old Ones before," she said reassuringly.

Stefan felt a surge of affection for Elena's friends: stepping up immediately, ready to protect her.

Jack gave a short laugh. "You've never killed one like Solomon," he said.

Stefan felt his fists clench. "You're surprisingly well informed," he snapped at the newcomer. "Who told you about Elena's blood?"

"We keep our ears close to the ground," Jack said. "When Old Ones started turning up dead and we figured out that blood had killed them, we were able to put that together with rumors about a new Guardian on the scene. Once we knew you existed, Elena, it wasn't hard to find you." Stefan, already tense, felt his canine teeth sharpening. He turned his back to the others and breathed deeply, gripping tight to the chair beside him, and, slowly, his teeth slipped back to normal.

"What's different about Solomon?" Elena was asking behind him. "Meredith is right—we've fought other Old Ones before. Klaus, Celine, Davos. They were all cunning and ruthless and terribly strong. They had to be, to survive as long as they did." Elena's voice was steady, but Stefan noticed the flash of panic in her deep blue eyes, the pink flush of her cheeks.

Jack leaned forward, his elbows resting on his knees. "We've been tracking Solomon for years. I've never even *seen* him, just evidence that he's been somewhere. Most of the Old Ones, they're flashy. They *want* hunters to see how powerful they are, to show that they're not afraid of us. Solomon, though, he keeps to himself." Jack spread his fingers wide. "He can get anywhere, do what he wants, and, by the time we figure where he was, he's long gone. He has more power than you can imagine, and he's always a few steps ahead of us." He paused. "We think Solomon won't stop until he's killed Elena."

Stefan automatically moved closer to Elena. "He's not the first one to try, and I'm still standing," she said, looking pale but stubborn.

"I want to help protect you," Jack said intently, his eyes locking with Elena's. "It's been my mission for so long to bring Solomon down. But I've never gotten close. I think if we band together"—he glanced at the others again—"we might have a shot at defeating him. Meredith, I know you haven't known many hunters outside your family. You've done so much on your own, and with Stefan—but you could do even more with a team of hunters backing you up."

"I had another hunter I worked with for a while. Samantha," Meredith said. "But she died. Vampires killed her." Her face seemed impassive, but Stefan had known Meredith long enough to notice the strain at the corners of her mouth when she thought of Samantha. There was a longing there, he knew. Like werewolves, hunters did best in a pack. Elena bumped her knee comfortingly against Meredith's.

"These rumors," Stefan asked, "how widespread are they? Even if we manage to kill Solomon, will there be other Old Ones coming after Elena? Should we be running instead of fighting?" He reached for Elena's hand, his fingers tightening protectively over hers.

Elena shook her head, squeezing his hand in return. "We can't run forever, Stefan," she murmured.

Jack interrupted, his voice brisk. "Like I said, I think Solomon is the last. I've been hunting all my life, and there aren't any other Old Ones I know of, not now that you"— he nodded to Stefan and Meredith—"have killed so many. So, are you with me?"

Matt, who'd been following the conversation in silence, gave a quick jerk of a nod. "Anything we can do against Solomon," he said, like a pledge. "We have to stop him before it all begins again."

"We can do this, Stefan," Meredith said, her gray eyes shining. "We've already tracked down and killed *three* Old Ones. If Solomon's coming to us, that just makes it more convenient." She grinned. "We won't have to travel."

Rubbing the bridge of his nose between his thumb and forefinger, Stefan thought carefully. "If hunting Solomon gets too dangerous for Elena, she and I will leave town," he told Jack. "Her safety is the most important thing." Jack nodded solemnly.

"We'll work as a team," Stefan went on slowly, "like we always do. Bonnie and Alaric can use magic—Bonnie, maybe you can ask Mrs. Flowers what she knows about divination for evil creatures?" Bonnie nodded at the mention of her elderly mentor back in Fell's Church. "Elena, keep your Guardian Powers on alert. If there's an Old One near Dalcrest, there ought to be some signs of evil you can pick up on." He let go of Elena and began to pace the room, his steps quickening as he thought. "Jack, we should get together with your team, figure out how we can best work together."

He crossed to the closet and pulled out his hunter's bag, trying to think what they would need. More vervain for Meredith's weapons, to keep Solomon and any other vampires he might have with him from clouding the humans' minds. Stakes of white ash. Iron.

He unzipped the bag, and for a moment his mind stopped, unable to process what he was seeing. There was a fine dust all over his weapons. Wood dust, he realized, soft under his hands except for a few small splinters. Something cut into his palm and he pulled it back quickly, wincing. It was a tiny shard of metal. There was an ache in his gums as his canines extended slowly, throbbing in time with his beating heart, and he realized that he was smelling blood. Elena's blood.

"My stave," he said, slowly. "It's—it's been destroyed."

He could hear his friends exclaiming, getting to their feet, Sammy meowing in complaint as Bonnie unceremoniously dumped him off her lap. They were crowding behind him, all but Jack, who was standing a little away from the rest of the group. Elena touched Stefan's arm gently. But his gaze was riveted on the pulverized remains of his best weapon against the Old Ones. Nothing else had been touched.

"He came right in," Stefan said, amazed. "Without being invited. All the safeguards and charms we have on this apartment, and somehow he knew where our only real weapon against him was hidden and came straight to it." He finally dragged his gaze away from the remains of his stave, and his eyes met Jack's. They were dark and full of what looked like pity.

"You see what I mean about Solomon," the hunter said softly. "He broke through all your protective charms like they were tissue paper and disappeared without a trace. This is what we're up against. This is what we have to fight." His voice grew somber. "This was a warning."

#TVD11WithoutaTrace

att was late meeting Jasmine. When he jogged around the corner, she was standing outside the little vintage movie theater, her arms wrapped around herself to ward off the chill of the late spring night.

A fierce, protective happiness lit up inside Matt at the sight of Jasmine. She glanced at her watch, clearly a little irritated—she didn't get much time off from her residency at the hospital—but she wouldn't be instinctively worried by Matt's lateness. Jasmine didn't automatically assume horrible things had happened. Because they never did, not to her.

Matt tried to shove aside the thoughts of Elena in danger, of Stefan's face that afternoon as he had gazed down at the remains of his stave. Now he was here, with Jasmine, in the normal world.

"Hey," he said, halting in front of her, panting a little. "I'm really sorry."

Jasmine crossed her eyes and stuck out her tongue at him. "Monster," she said sweetly. "The only way you can make it up to me is by buying me a very large popcorn and getting lots of fake butter."

As they waited in line at the concession stand, Matt wrapped his arms around Jasmine's shoulders, and she reached up to twine the fingers of her hand with his. "So what held you up?" she asked. "It's not like you to be late." Her big brown eyes fixed on his expectantly.

Matt froze. He hadn't thought about what to tell her. His silence was long enough that Jasmine's eyebrows rose slightly.

"Elena was in a car accident," he blurted, not lying, but not telling the whole truth.

Jasmine gasped, pressing her free hand against her mouth. "Oh my God," she said. "Is she okay?"

"Oh, yeah, she's fine, but she got a little banged up," Matt said, and then hurriedly corrected himself, remembering how Stefan's blood had healed Elena. Jasmine was a doctor; she would want to see Elena's injuries. "I mean, she's okay, but her car got pretty banged up. She hit a telephone pole."

They ordered popcorn and sodas and headed into the theater.

"That's terrifying. How did she manage to hit a telephone pole?" Jasmine asked as they settled into their seats, her hand still in his. Her eyes narrowed suspiciously. "Wait, was she on the phone? I told her, driving while using a phone is just as dangerous as driving drunk."

"No, I don't think she was on the phone," Matt said, although he wasn't sure.

"Well, what happened, then?" Jasmine asked again. Matt could feel himself stiffening and rolled his neck to let go of the tension building up in him. It wasn't Jasmine's fault he didn't know what to tell her about Elena's accident; these were perfectly natural questions.

"Elena wasn't *drinking*, was she?" Jasmine asked him, her forehead crinkling.

"No! God!" Matt said. "There's nothing to tell. It was just a normal accident, and we're going to make sure it doesn't happen again." A woman in the row ahead turned to look at them, and Matt realized his voice had risen.

"What do you mean you're going to make sure it doesn't happen again?" Jasmine asked in a low, persistent voice.

For one crazy moment, Matt wondered if maybe he could tell Jasmine the truth. She wouldn't believe him at first—no one would. But he guessed she'd probably noticed things that didn't quite add up about them in the past. And she cared about all his friends. If he shared some of the worries that weighed him down, maybe Jasmine could help him bear them.

Something in him immediately recoiled from the idea. It was selfish of him to even consider it. Jasmine existed outside of all the violence and fear that had been Matt's life ever since high school, ever since the Salvatore brothers had first come to Fell's Church. She reminded Matt of the way he'd been before this all started.

Everything they had suffered—Elena's death, Klaus's attacks, hunting the Old Ones—had marked Matt and all his friends. Even Bonnie, the sweetest of them, had something hard-edged and fierce about her now. This new toughness had saved their lives more than once. But he didn't want Jasmine to have to change like that.

"I don't know," he told her. "I don't know why I said that. It was an accident."

Jasmine turned to look carefully into his face, then frowned, clearly aware that he was hiding something. She'd let go of his hand, Matt realized, and his fingers felt cold without hers.

Matt clenched his jaw, swallowing his urge to beg her forgiveness, tell her everything. But then he thought of what could happen. Chloe had *died* because of her involvement in the mess of vampires and werewolves, warriors and demons that Matt's life had become. Even if Jasmine resented him for it, he would never tell her. He would keep her safe, no matter what.

* * *

"Duck!" Bonnie shouted wildly, scrunching down as far as she could in the passenger seat of the car.

"I can't duck; I'm driving," Zander said calmly. "Anyway, your parents aren't going to see us."

Bonnie sat up and turned in her seat to look back at her parents' house. There was no car in the drive; they must be out. "I just feel guilty, coming to Fell's Church and not letting them know," she said.

"You're on a very important mission," Zander told her. "Anyway, we're having dinner with them next week."

"I know," Bonnie said. "I just hope Mrs. Flowers has some ideas about how to search for Solomon. Elena's Powers aren't picking up anything." The elderly, powerful witch had taught Bonnie a lot of what she knew.

"Hmm," Zander responded, taking a left toward Mrs. Flowers's house. Bonnie's eyes drifted to his arm muscles flexing beneath his golden-tanned skin. Werewolves were naturally strong, of course, but ever since Zander and a couple of his Packmates had started a landscaping business after college, he'd only gotten buffer. She sighed appreciatively.

"There's a car in Mrs. Flowers's drive," Zander said curiously as they pulled up. Bonnie blinked; there was a car, a shiny little blue Honda. That was strange. Mrs. Flowers was basically a recluse and, anyway, she had known Bonnie and Zander were coming.

"Maybe it's somebody selling something?" Bonnie wondered aloud as they trailed through the untidy herb garden and up the path to the front door.

In the kitchen, they found Mrs. Flowers sipping tea with a girl about their own age. She didn't *look* like she was selling anything: She was as tiny as Bonnie herself, dressed in a T-shirt and jeans, with wild curly blond hair and a spattering of freckles across her cheeks.

"Hey!" the girl said as soon as she saw them. She put her teacup down a little too hard, sloshing tea into the saucer and onto the table. "Oops," she added, grinning.

"Hello, children," Mrs. Flowers said serenely. "Help yourself to some scones. Alysia, if you look behind you, you'll see napkins to wipe up that spill."

They settled at the table, Bonnie squirming impatiently as Mrs. Flowers poured two more cups of tea and handed around plates for scones and little sandwiches. She needed to talk to Mrs. Flowers about serious business, but Bonnie couldn't see a way to bring up the subject of Old Ones in front of this stranger. And who was she, anyway?

From across the table, Alysia kept smiling at her. Bonnie shifted uncomfortably. Next to her, Zander bit happily into a scone. "These are amazing," he told Mrs. Flowers, who smiled at him.

"Um," Bonnie began, growing impatient, "Mrs. Flowers, did you manage to find anything on the . . . problem I called you about?"

"There are some books of protection charms and divination spells on the table in the hall," Mrs. Flowers said briskly. "You may take them with you when you leave. I'm afraid, though, that I don't think the spells will do anything Elena can't do on her own." She put down her teacup and looked at Bonnie seriously, her blue eyes sharp. "I think Alysia might be able to assist you, though. She works with a group that could help you strengthen your Power."

"What kind of a group?" Bonnie asked, confused.

Alysia straightened, her voice becoming formal, as if she was reciting a prepared speech. "It's nice to meet you, Bonnie," she began. "I represent an association of people who work together through the manipulation of natural forces to oppose negative elements. Mrs. Flowers is"—she shared a look with the older woman—"one of the chief contacts of our group, and she's recommended that we invite you to join us." The girl smiled eagerly, making her look even younger. "She had a lot of good things to say about you, Bonnie. You sound like one of the most talented recruits we've come across."

"What do you mean, 'recruits'?" Bonnie asked suspiciously. "What exactly are you recruiting me for?"

Alysia flushed pink to the tips of her ears. "I'm sorry," she said. "I should have explained better. This is the first time I've coordinated a gathering. We'd like to invite you to our retreat for a few weeks, to share your abilities with others who have a deep connection to the natural elements, and they'll share their talents with you. If you find it useful, you can come back every year or two and work with the same team. We all help one another focus and hone our abilities. We're stronger when we work together."

"Like . . . a workshop?" Bonnie asked.

"Sort of," Alysia agreed, dropping the formal tone. "We're really just a bunch of people who have magic powers and good intentions, and we think that if we work together we can get stronger, and counter some of the bad things in the world."

"Oh," Bonnie managed. She wasn't sure what to say. It sounded like a good idea, but did she really have time to join—what was this, a coven? "I've never really worked with anyone else. Except for Mrs. Flowers, of course."

"It'll just be for a few weeks. And I can guarantee it's a great way to take your abilities to the next level. Watch."

Alysia raised her hand and, her forehead wrinkling in concentration, made a complicated gesture, too quick for Bonnie to follow. There was a flash of red, and Bonnie heard birdsong as something fluttered past her, disappearing near Mrs. Flowers's china cabinet. Shadows of vines spread across the wall, and the scent of flowers and warm rain blossomed all around them. In the middle of Mrs. Flowers's kitchen, Alysia had conjured up a pocket of tropical rain forest.

"Wow," Bonnie said, as the illusion faded and the normal kitchen reassembled around them. "That was really neat."

"I'm good with illusions," Alysia said, shrugging. "But I never could have done that before I met the others."

"It sounds interesting," Bonnie said carefully. "Would you mind, though, if I checked something out for myself? No offense, Mrs. Flowers."

The older woman waved away the disclaimer. "I understand perfectly, my dear," she said.

"Don't be scared," Bonnie told Alysia, then turned to Zander. "Can you see if she's telling the truth?"

Zander got to his feet, accidentally jostling the table so that the delicate cups rattled, and took a deep breath. Then suddenly his body twisted, his face lengthening into a snout, his hands forming into claws. Alysia gave a startled yelp. In just a few seconds, a huge, beautiful white wolf stood beside them, gazing intently at Alysia with his sky-blue eyes.

"Oh, my God," Alysia said faintly, scooting her chair back from the table. Her face had paled so that the freckles stood out like little dark dots.

"Just stay still for a minute," Bonnie said. "He won't hurt you."

Zander walked around the table to sniff at Alysia, his furred jaw almost pressing against hers.

"Is everything you've told me the truth?" Bonnie asked. Alysia nodded. "You have to answer out loud," Bonnie added gently.

"Y-yes." Alysia's voice shook.

"Do you have any evil intent toward me?"

"No."

Zander changed back—always, Bonnie thought, a less painful-looking process than turning into a wolf—and rolled his shoulders, stretching. "She's good," he told Bonnie.

Alysia had her hand pressed against her chest and was breathing hard. "Oh my God," she gasped. "You control a werewolf?"

"What? No," Bonnie said. "I don't *control* him."

"Don't listen to her," Zander said affably. "She totally owns me."

"It sounds good," Bonnie said, ignoring her boyfriend. "I'd like to be able to channel more Power." She hated to admit it, even to herself, but she'd sort of plateaued—she was handy with herbs and charms, and could work a finding or protection spell pretty well, but her Power hadn't grown much in the last few years. "When does it start?"

"Tomorrow," Alysia said. "I know it's short notice, but we had some trouble getting the whole group that we wanted together."

"Tomorrow?" Bonnie shook her head, giving an incredulous little laugh. "I can't. I have a job. And Elena's in danger; I can't leave her now."

Mrs. Flowers's lips thinned. "Your best chance of helping Elena is by expanding your Power. You need to give this serious consideration, Bonnie."

"I don't—tomorrow's too soon," Bonnie said.

"I think you should go," Zander broke in unexpectedly. Bonnie turned to stare at him.

"You do?" she asked.

"Yeah," he said. "I mean, obviously, I'd miss you like crazy, but this seems like something you need to do. You owe it to yourself to try. And the school year just ended, so you have time off work."

Zander was right. Bonnie envisioned herself full of Power, protecting Elena, protecting everyone. In her imagination, she waved one hand and a shimmering, clear wall came down around her friends, separating them from danger.

She thought of how she'd felt the other day—that no one needed her, that she wasn't useful anymore in protecting Dalcrest from the supernatural. This was her chance.

"Okay," she said, turning to Alysia, who clapped her hands and smiled. Mrs. Flowers nodded approvingly. "I'm in."

9

"I can't believe Bonnie just took off like that," Elena said, swinging Stefan's hand as they walked. They'd had lunch with Meredith, but then she had gone to the law library to do some studying—law school seemed to mean constant deadlines—and now they were heading back to their apartment alone. Zander had driven Bonnie to the airport that morning.

"She'll be back," Stefan said. Bonnie had left them with as many safety provisions as she could: charm bags for their cars and apartments, herb mixtures to drink or scatter for protection. She must have been up all night making them.

"I know. But I'll still miss her." Elena leaned against Stefan for a moment. "I just worry that someday . . . I'll lose her for good. And Aunt Judith told me the house is officially listed with the realtor now. She's looking for a place in Richmond."

"Bonnie will be back," Stefan said reassuringly. "And your family won't be far away."

"I know," Elena said, sighing. "But can you indulge my self-pity, please?"

"I'll indulge." Stefan tugged her closer as they reached the building. "Let me distract you for a while. Tell me what we'll do once we get rid of Solomon."

Hand in hand, they wandered through the double doors of their apartment building and started up the two flights of stairs.

"I'd like to go back to Paris," Elena said dreamily. "I spent the summer there just before we met, did you know that?"

Stefan, putting his key in the door, was about to answer—of course he knew that, he remembered everything Elena had ever told him, everything he'd ever been told about her—when he stopped.

"Stefan, what's wrong?" Elena asked, sounding worried, and he held up his hand to quiet her. He smelled blood.

"Stay here." He heard Elena's heart begin to pound faster, and he squeezed her hand reassuringly before letting go. "There's blood in there. I need to check it out." He carefully opened the front door and went inside. Everything looked normal, but the scent of blood grew stronger. Elena gave a faint, choked-off cry, and he knew that she could smell it now, too.

Gesturing at her to stay back, Stefan crept silently toward the kitchen, staying close to the wall. He sent tendrils of

Power through the apartment, but found nothing—no one, human or otherwise, inside. But the smell of blood was overwhelming, hot and sticky and flooding through his senses. He felt his canines lengthening, beginning to ache, and his senses sharpened.

There were drops of blood scattered across the kitchen floor, leading toward the closed bedroom door.

Not just drops, he realized, as his heart sank. Paw prints.

Stefan swung open the bedroom door and the smells of blood, of *pain*, hit him like a physical blow. There was something small and pale on the bed. Blood was spattered across the comforter, leaving it soaking wet and dark red in places. The pale thing, Stefan realized, was Sammy. Their cat had been torn to pieces, his white fur matted with gore.

"Stefan?" Elena's voice reached him from the kitchen.

"Wait—" he said, but it was too late. A soft, hurt cry burst from Elena as she stepped inside. She rushed to the bed, to the sad remains of her pet.

"Elena!" Stefan said. "Don't look."

But Elena shook her head and stretched out a hand, carefully touching Sammy's head with one finger. The blood was dripping—Stefan could hear it falling off the comforter to pool on the floor. "Who would have done this?" Elena asked, tears running down her face. "He was just a harmless cat."

"Elena," Stefan whispered in warning, pulling her close to him. Something was very wrong.

With a loud crack, the windows began to frost over. The mirror turned silver with ice. Elena shuddered, and Stefan could see her breath coming in small clouds of vapor.

"What's happening?" she whispered. Stefan just held tight to her. He wanted to protect her, but how could he when he didn't know what they were facing? He turned toward the door, but that was freezing over, too, the lock encased in frost.

Everything was turning to ice, even the pool of blood on the floor hardening at the edges. As Stefan looked around helplessly, the ice over the windows and mirror gave a loud snap and split from top to bottom, the cracks forming a jagged *S*.

In the sudden stillness, Stefan and Elena stared at each other, shocked. Her face was pale, her lapis lazuli eyes wide with terror.

"Solomon," she said, her voice shaking. "*S* is for Solomon. He's been here again."

#TVD11SolomonWasHere

* * *

The walls were dripping. Matt wiped the floor below the kitchen window with a dish towel, but the long trails of water from the melting ice had streaked the paint all the way down the wall. It was too big a mess to fix with a few minutes and a towel. After swiping at it a few times, he gave up and settled for taking a cup of tea out to Elena.

She was sitting on the sofa between Stefan and Meredith, a blanket wrapped around her shoulders. "Thanks," she said weakly when he handed her the cup. Matt had known Elena long enough to see that her eyes were bright with unshed tears. Poor little Sammy's body had been tucked into a box by the front door; they would bury him tomorrow when it was light out.

Alaric and Zander came back in the front door of the apartment, the door banging behind them. They'd been patrolling the halls of Stefan and Elena's building, checking to see if there were any other signs of Solomon's invasion.

"Not a whiff of a scent," Zander said, in response to the others' anxious looks. "And no one I talked to had seen any strangers."

Alaric carried a small brass triangle, from which hung a crystal on a chain. He tilted it from one side to the other, the crystal swinging, then shook his head. "There's nothing paranormal resonating anywhere in the building, so far as I can tell," he said. "Not even in here."

"Jack said that Solomon could go anywhere without leaving a trace," Meredith said.

"Are we sure it was him?" Matt asked, his gaze drawn to the sad box by the door. "I don't understand how he's getting in and out of the apartment. No one invited him."

Elena drew her knees up and wrapped her arms around them, resting her pointed chin on top. "I don't know," she said. "But who else could it be? In some ways, it's more frightening to think that we might have *two* enemies."

"Or maybe," Matt began, hesitant, "maybe he doesn't need to be invited."

They all fell silent as the implication sank in. If Solomon could come into their homes without an invitation, then the normal rules that governed vampires didn't apply to him. Nowhere was safe.

There was a soft knock on the door. Zander answered it, his usually genial expression tense and wary. If he'd been in wolf form, Matt thought, the fur on his hackles would have been bristling.

"It's Jack and his team," Stefan told him, rising to greet them, and Zander stepped back to let them enter.

"Thanks for coming so quickly," Stefan said, clasping Jack's hand. He gestured back toward Matt and the others. "We haven't found anything yet."

Jack's face was grim. "Meet my team. This is Roy, and Alex"—two tall dark-haired men who might have been brothers each raised a hand in greeting—"Darlene"—an Asian woman probably in her thirties smiled tightly at them—"and Trinity." Trinity, younger than the others, had light brown shoulder-length hair and large blue eyes. She gave a dorky little wave when Jack introduced her.

They were all different physically, but Matt thought that he would have recognized them as hunters without being told. They shared a kind of competent grace, as if they were fully in control of what every part of their bodies was doing at any time. They all had those wary, alert eyes that took in everyone in the room.

"Give me all the details," Jack said, looking at Meredith. She told him in just a few sentences about the slaughter of Elena's cat and the ice that had cracked to reveal the letter *S*.

"Thank you, that was very clear," Jack said approvingly. Meredith's olive cheeks flushed slightly with pleasure, and Matt felt his eyebrows lifting. It wasn't like cool, suspicious Meredith to care what a newcomer thought of her.

Then again, Meredith was a hunter by nature. Her parents had cut off contact with others of their kind when they stopped hunting themselves. Of course Meredith would be excited to finally meet more hunters.

"Are you sure it was Solomon?" Elena asked. "You said he wasn't flashy like the other Old Ones, that he hardly left a trace. This was flashy, and took a lot of Power. And the blood . . ." Her voice trailed off unhappily, and she twisted the edge of her shirt between her fingers.

The young brown-haired hunter named Trinity knelt down next to Elena. "I'm so sorry about your pet," she said sympathetically, laying her hand on Elena's arm and stilling her anxious movement. Trinity's eyes were warm with sympathy. Elena smiled weakly at her.

"It's definitely Solomon," Jack said. "You're right; he doesn't usually show off like this. As long as I've been tracking him, he's managed to be practically invisible."

"He doesn't even leave bodies behind," Darlene added. "People just disappear into thin air if he wants them to. He doesn't typically leave any evidence at all."

"So he *wanted* you to know he was here," Jack said. "He's sending you a clear message. He wants you to know he's after you."

"I have tracking Powers," Elena said. "Usually. But I haven't been able to find him."

"I wish Bonnie were here," Zander said. "Maybe she could do a spell that would show us something."

But Jack was shaking his head. "We've tried magic," he said. "Somehow Solomon's able to block it. It's like he's invisible and intangible to every sense we have, even the magical ones."

"How can we search for someone who's invisible?" Meredith snapped. Her hands had balled into fists, and she looked ready to leap up and start fighting.

"I wish I knew," Jack said, sighing.

"There's a funny smell in here," Zander said suddenly, cocking his head.

"Blood?" Matt asked. He could smell the coppery scent of blood throughout the apartment, and it was making him feel sick.

Zander shot him a wry look. "Something else," he said, prowling across the living room to the kitchen, sniffing. "Over here, maybe," he said, sticking his head through the kitchen doorway.

"I don't smell it," Stefan said, following him. He said it mildly, though: They all knew that Zander's sense of smell was stronger than anyone's, even Stefan's.

In the doorway between the kitchen and bedroom, Zander bent down and scraped his nails across the floor, then straightened and brushed something into his palm. "Huh," he said. Matt craned forward to see what looked like plain old dirt in Zander's hand.

"What is it?" he asked.

Zander looked up, then came back into the living room, his hand extended. "It smells like apples," he said.

"There's that apple orchard to the west of town," Matt said thoughtfully. "Have you guys been there lately?" Stefan and Elena shook their heads.

"Could it be a clue?" Zander said, looking hopeful.

Jack's eyes widened, then he grinned and slapped Zander on the back. "Maybe what we needed was a werewolf's nose," he said. "Looks like we're going apple-picking tomorrow."

eredith flipped her pillow over to find its cooler side, lay down again, and squeezed her eyes shut. *Sleep*, she told herself firmly. She had so much to do tomorrow, so much to do every day. She couldn't afford not to be rested.

But when she closed her eyes, all she saw was the cat's little body, bloody and torn. It was a message, she knew: Solomon wanted them to know it could have been any of them. Would be one of them, all of them, soon.

They were determined to find him, but so far Jack was right. Solomon seemed to be invisible.

They'd gone to the apple orchard and searched the fields and woods around it, hoping that Solomon's hideout would be nearby. Nothing. A heavy ominous feeling hung over all of them like a dark cloud. He was coming, and it would be better to hunt him and fight him on their own terms rather than wait for his attack.

Meredith flipped her pillow again and turned over, looking for a more comfortable position. Alaric was snoring softly next to her, sleeping like a log. Closing her eyes again, she saw white on red: the white cat ripped apart on the blood-drenched bed.

Then the image morphed into her friend Samantha, torn apart by vampires back in college, blood sprayed across her bed, and Meredith took a quick breath, one that sounded more like a sob to her own ears. Then it was her brother, Cristian, his gray eyes half-open, Meredith's own stave through his heart.

Every night recently it had been like this, images of death keeping Meredith awake until exhaustion finally caught up with her. So much death.

Pushing the memories away, she tried to make herself relax, timing her breathing to Alaric's: slow, long, steady breaths. She was so tired.

Time passed. After a while, she realized with a start that she was somewhere new. It was chilly, and a glaring white light hung above her, hurting her eyes. She tried to turn her face away.

She couldn't move.

Tensing her whole body, she took a deep breath and tried again. She still couldn't move. It felt like a tracery of thin wires was fitted over her body, holding her in place. Trying not to panic, Meredith strained against it, making an effort to lift one leg and then the other, her mouth dry with fear. Paralyzed.

Her heart thumped in her chest. She couldn't even turn her head. Meredith could hear herself panting, the sound harsh in the silence. Losing her careful control for a moment, she struggled frantically, the tendons in her neck going tight as she tried to thrash against the pillow. She wanted to hit out with her arms, kick, jump up and fight, or run away. But finally she stopped. She still couldn't move.

Calm down, she told herself sternly. *Figure out where you are.*

The light was blinding, making her eyes sting and water. But if she blinked away the tears, she could make out white walls, flat and sterile looking. A harsh antiseptic smell. Was she in a hospital?

Meredith was stretched out flat on some kind of bed or table, legs together, arms at her sides. There was something made of shiny silver metal just to the left of her head. She tried to examine it through the corner of her eyes. A sink maybe, or some kind of medical equipment.

Something moved at the edge of her field of vision, and she flinched backward. Whatever it was, she knew it wasn't good.

It was *watching* her.

Something in Meredith snapped, and she began to thrash again, straining ineffectively against the wires holding her immobilized. She tried to shut her eyes against the glare and found that they, too, were held open now. Her throat felt rough and raw, and a harsh, shrill sound went on and on, hurting her ears.

It was a while before she realized that she was the one screaming.

* * *

Meredith's eyes snapped open onto darkness. She gasped and panted, trying to calm her racing heart. She was in her own bed. *Just a dream.*

She'd kicked off the covers. Alaric was stirring and grumbling next to her. "S'matter?" he asked groggily. "You all right?"

"Bad dream," Meredith said, wiping roughly at her eyes. Hunters did *not* cry. "I couldn't move," she told him. "Something terrible was about to happen to me. I was . . ." She paused to gather her thoughts, and Alaric wrapped an arm around her, pulling her closer.

"It's okay," he murmured, his breath warm against her cheek. "Just a dream." He sighed, already falling back asleep. Meredith bit back more explanations of exactly how terrible the dream had been, how shaken and uncertain she still felt. Alaric was right; it was only a dream.

But she couldn't shake the feeling of dread coursing through her. There was only one person who might know what it meant, who took dreams as seriously as she did. *I wish Bonnie were here*, she thought longingly.

* * *

I wish I were home, Bonnie thought longingly. This was nothing at all like she'd pictured.

She'd thought a witchy retreat would be all about getting in touch with nature. Hadn't Alysia said that they would be channeling natural elements? Bonnie had pictured a bunch of earthy, hippie types, chanting and waving crystals in between learning about herbs and spells.

It wasn't anything like that. Instead, Bonnie found herself in an elegant skyscraper apartment far above the streets of Chicago. Looking out the floor-to-ceiling stretch of windows beside her, she could see a steady stream of traffic below, the cars tiny and toylike. There were about twenty people scattered in groups around the big room, all beautifully dressed, glasses in hand. Near her, a sharp-featured blonde in an ice-blue cocktail dress tipped her head back and laughed shrilly. It was an expensive cocktail party in a big city, and Bonnie felt frumpy and out of place.

I am strong, she told herself. *I am magic.* But she could feel a prickle of tears at the back of her eyes. This room of strangers felt almost like the glamorous high society she'd mingled with in the Dark Dimension, a place Bonnie had tried to shut away in the back of her mind. These people could easily be vampires and demons. Why not? What proof did she have, after all, that they weren't? There was no Lady Ulma here to dress Bonnie in finery so that she could outshine them all, and no Damon to save her if they trapped her. Bonnie shoved her fists deep into the pockets of her pants and hunched her shoulders.

The only thing that indicated this place might be more than just an expensive apartment was the mosaic floor, the small tiles underfoot making up a design of intertwining plants, with dark green and rich gold and patches of bright color. *Chamomile*, she identified automatically, *good for strength and healing. Valerian, to guard against evil. Daisies for happiness.*

The pattern of leaves and vines and blossoms went all the way around the edges of the room. Further in were runes and other symbols. All the ones she could identify were positive, signs of healing and protection. The center of the mosaic was filled by a brilliant golden sun.

So, probably good witches, Bonnie thought hopefully. *Not vampires and demons.*

Her phone buzzed in her bag, and Bonnie automatically fished it out. There was a text from Zander: *Remember you've saved the world before. You rock. Have fun. I <3 u. xox*

So sweet, Bonnie thought. He was thinking of her, had known she might be feeling nervous. She pictured Zander's eyes, the warm blue of a Caribbean sea, looking at her with simple love. Zander *believed* in her. And she should, too.

Bonnie straightened her shoulders and dropped the phone back in her bag before striding confidently into the middle of the room. *I've saved the world before. I rock.*

Alysia came over to meet her. In a little black dress, her wild curls tamed in a loose bun, she was more pulled together than she'd been at Mrs. Flowers's. But her wide, freckly smile was the same.

"Bonnie!" she exclaimed, handing her a glass of wine. "Let me introduce you to the people you'll be working with over the next few weeks." She led her to a small group centered around a leather sofa. The floor beneath them, Bonnie noted, had the Nordic rune Fehu. The slanty *F* represented abundance, success, and energy. *I guess Mrs. Flowers making me memorize all those runes might come in handy after all*, she thought.

There were three other people in what was going to be her group. On the couch was a thin African American man a few years older than Bonnie whom Alysia introduced as Rick, and a gray-haired older woman named Marilise. Poppy, a tall, willowy girl whose designer clothes screamed "society diva" to Bonnie, hovered beside them.

After introducing them all, Alysia left to talk to another group, and an awkward silence stretched between them. Bonnie fiddled with the glass in her hand, putting it down on a tiny table at one end of the couch, then picking it up again.

"So," Rick offered at last with a thin smile, "is this what you guys were expecting?"

Marilise shook her head. "I'm used to pulling energy out of the elements when I work," she said. "I like to have my feet planted firmly on the ground and growing things all around me. I don't know how I'm going to manage."

Poppy was nodding eagerly. "I totally agree," she said. "I talked to Alysia about it, asked her why they brought us all to the middle of Chicago. She said part of the challenge is connecting with natural elements anywhere, even in places that are the farthest from nature. It's supposed to make us stronger," she finished with an awkward little laugh.

They're all just as nervous as I am, Bonnie realized, and that fact warmed her. She smiled at Poppy and the girl grinned back at her, tucking a tiny wisp of hair back into place.

"I've never really thought of the things I can do as connecting with the natural elements," Bonnie said thoughtfully, "but nature's all around us, isn't it? Even here. We've got the sun and the wind, and the earth's still *there*, under all that concrete." They were all nodding, and Bonnie stood up straighter under their attention. "I use a lot of herbs," she told them, "and those are a bit of the natural world you can take anywhere."

Looking at their interested faces, Bonnie realized that here were people who wanted to learn what she had to teach them, who could probably teach her things she didn't know. *Zander was right*, she thought. She smiled tentatively around at the group, and they smiled back at her. *Right now, this is where I need to be.*

11

"**I**s that a *gun?*" Elena asked, knowing it was a stupid question. They were at the apple orchard on the edge of town, on the roof of the building that housed the cider press, and Jack was loading a handgun with wooden bullets, quickly and competently. What Elena *meant* was, why do you have a gun?

"Sure," Jack said easily. Catching Elena's expression, he laughed. "Look, I know that bullets won't stop a vampire, especially not an Old One. But wooden bullets might slow him down a little at a distance while we're getting ready to fight."

"Good idea," Stefan said thoughtfully, resting a hand on Elena's shoulder. "What else do you use?"

"Take a look," Jack said, nodding toward a couple of large duffle bags in the corner. Meredith and Zander were already picking carefully through them, examining weapons, while Alaric watched from a few feet away.

"Is this a flamethrower?" Meredith asked, her gray eyes bright with excitement. "Awesome!"

The roof of the cider press building was shady and cool. "We haven't seen a sign of Solomon," Jack had told them when his team welcomed them up. "But we're keeping an eye on things. This is a good place to train, too. Nothing overlooks us, plenty of room, and there aren't many people here this time of year. Easy to avoid being seen."

It should have been a peaceful place, the tiny green apples dangling from the trees' branches, no sound but the rustling of the leaves. But shadows lurked beneath the trees, and Elena shuddered. What did this sun-dappled place have to do with an ancient vampire?

She watched, slightly wary, as Darlene handed Meredith something that looked like a weed sprayer attached to a couple of cylinders and Meredith shot a ball of flame across the roof.

"Careful there," Darlene warned, but Meredith laughed.

"That's such a good idea," she said. "Take the fire right to the vampire. How did you manage to get that?"

"We've got connections," Jack said with a wink. Then he sobered. "Seriously, though, there's nothing more important than eliminating vampires. Vampires who are a threat to humanity, of course," he added quickly, looking at Stefan.

"You want to see some of the fighting moves we've worked out?" Trinity offered eagerly. At Meredith's nod, Trinity picked up a stave from the bag and took a tae kwon do stance, poised with one foot in front of the other, her weight carefully balanced. "Attack me," she said, smiling broadly. "But not with the flamethrower, please."

Meredith flashed her a smile in response, and slipped out her own stave. Before Trinity could brace herself, Meredith swept the stave at her legs, and Trinity had to leap to avoid the blow. A moment later, Roy, the shorter of the two brothers, joined in, swinging a heavy blade at Meredith's arms.

"Practice sword; it's blunt," Jack muttered in an aside to Elena.

Stefan joined the fight, moving so quickly and gracefully that he seemed like a blur, using his superior strength to pull Trinity off balance as his teeth just grazed her throat. But then Alex, the other dark-haired brother, jumped in. The three hunters managed to separate Meredith and Stefan, blocking them whenever either got close to one of their opponents. Alex fell to one knee as Meredith swung her stave at his head, and Trinity immediately stepped on his back, launching herself into the air and knocking Meredith to the ground.

The three hunters were fighting smoothly as a unit, keeping Meredith and Stefan off balance. It reminded Elena of how the Pack fought, and she glanced at Zander. He was watching with a smile of simple enjoyment, his eyes sharp.

"Nice," Meredith said, waving away the hand Trinity extended to her and climbing to her feet.

"We know you two fight well together," Jack said, nodding to Stefan. "You could never have defeated Old Ones if you didn't. But we hunters have our own techniques, based on centuries of experience fighting in groups. We can teach you, if you want."

He and Darlene lined up across from Meredith and Stefan, beginning to demonstrate stances and holds. Trinity wandered over to Elena.

"Want to spar?" she offered, grinning easily and pushing her long brown hair out of her eyes.

Elena felt herself flush. "Thanks," she said, "but I'm not a fighter."

"That's not what *I* heard," Trinity argued. "You're a Principal, aren't you? Come on. Want me to show you some moves?"

Elena reconsidered. Since she'd met Stefan, she'd found herself fighting against all kinds of enemies—supernatural and otherwise—and there was always the chance that one day her Guardian Powers and her friends wouldn't be enough to save her in a battle. Maybe it *was* time she learned to defend herself better. Plus there was the edge of a challenge in Trinity's cheerful gaze.

"You're on," Elena said. "How do we start?"

Trinity's smile spread. "Okay, slide your feet shoulder-width apart, and balance your weight equally between them. Keep your arms loose with your fists just in front of your stomach." She glanced down and nudged Elena's feet a little closer together with her own sneakered foot. "Good," she said. "Now, just react as I move at you."

She punched straight at Elena's chest, moving in half time, and Elena lifted her arm automatically to block the blow. "Good," Trinity said again, shifting quickly to kick at Elena. She made contact this time, her foot gently hitting the side of Elena's thigh.

Elena swung around and kicked back at her automatically. Trinity dodged out of the way, huffing a small surprised laugh. "Awesome," she said. "Powerful and amazing, right? Try again, but this time, slide your right foot a bit forward and point your left foot to the side. That way, you can shift your weight back better when you kick and get more momentum going."

Elena changed her foot position and was eyeing Trinity carefully, getting ready to kick again, when Zander stiffened and held up a hand for silence. "There's someone coming. More than one person," he said. "Apple smell's stronger."

Stefan heard them, too; Elena could tell. He and Zander stepped to either side of the roof entrance, ready.

"Come on," Trinity whispered, as she and the other human hunters arranged themselves in a curving line to meet whatever came through the door. Elena and Alaric, the weakest fighters, dropped back behind the line. Alaric was muttering a quick charm, and Elena closed her eyes for a moment, searching for evil. She couldn't activate her Guardian Powers without an immediate threat. At least, not yet.

But, try as she might, she couldn't sense anything unusual. Then the roof door burst open and three figures charged through.

They looked like a bunch of townie dads, Elena had time to think, but it didn't matter. She'd seen enough vampires to know they could have started out as anyone. Two had stakes, and one carried a machete, its blade gleaming wickedly.

The one with the machete swung it at Stefan, his teeth bared with rage, and Elena gasped in surprise as Stefan jerked back, blood streaming down his arm. Zander tackled Stefan's attacker from behind, low and fast, changing forms as he cannoned into the back of the guy's legs, and they fell in a tangle of fur and limbs. The machete clattered onto the rooftop beside them.

Stefan, his wound already closing, grabbed the next attacker by the arm and flung him in the air like a rag doll. The guy landed with a thud at the edge of the roof as

Meredith stepped smoothly forward to strike him with her stave. At the edge of the roof, Jack drew his gun.

The third man, tall and blond, reached for the machete, swinging it up with an easy grip. Jack fired his gun, but the man kept coming, machete raised in one hand and a stake in the other.

"Wait!" Stefan called. "Stop!" He was staring in horror at the guy he had thrown across the roof, who was clambering to his feet slowly, blood streaming down his face from a head wound. The man with the machete snarled and charged toward Meredith, his shirt darkening with his own blood.

Stefan reached out and held him back, pinning his arms and forcing the man to drop the machete and the stake. Zander held his opponent by the back of the throat and shook him a little, growling.

"They're *humans*," Stefan said. "They've been Influenced; they're not responsible for what they're doing."

The blood-soaked guy charged, but Jack grabbed him and held his arms firmly behind his back, as he struggled and kicked. All three kept fighting without pause, wrenching away from their captors ceaselessly, even though they were clearly helpless against them. Elena could see now what Stefan had sensed with his Power: Their auras were curiously clouded, as if they weren't really aware of what was happening.

"What should we do?" Trinity asked, distressed.

"Let me try," Stefan said. He shifted so that he was holding the blond guy firmly still, face-to-face. The man snarled and tried to lunge at him, not flinching even when Stefan dug his fist into the bleeding bullet wound to stop him. Elena saw Stefan's gaze flicker down to the wound and back again, the almost imperceptible flare of his nostrils as the scent of fresh blood hit him. Then he swallowed and focused, locking his eyes on the guy's.

"You don't want to do this," he said softly. "You want to stop and go home." He was trying to use his Power to break the Influence, Elena could tell, but it wasn't working. The man's aura grew grayer and more clouded as Stefan spoke, and he fought harder against him. Stefan tried using his Power on the others, one after the other, but it was no use.

"I can't break it," he admitted finally. "They've been Influenced by someone really Powerful."

Jack nodded. "Solomon. He's sending you a message. He knew we wouldn't kill the humans, and that they couldn't beat us. He wanted to show you how Powerful he is."

"I've got an idea," Zander said thoughtfully. Back in human form, he rubbed at his jaw as if it were sore, working it slowly. "I might be able to break the compulsion enough to get these guys to tell us the truth." He turned the bearded man with the head wound to face him, keeping a steady, gentle grip on him. Zander was so laid-back, Elena sometimes forgot how inhumanly strong he was. But now she couldn't help seeing how easily Zander controlled his captive, even though the guy fought and thrashed, his eyes stretching wide and his teeth bared.

Zander rested his chin on the guy's shoulder and wrapped his arms around him, pressing their chests together. Turning his head to face into his captive's neck, he breathed steadily and deeply. After a moment, Elena realized Zander was growling softly, deep in his throat.

At first, the guy fought harder, rearing away, but Zander only pulled him closer, blood from his face smearing across Zander's own cheek. The hair on Zander's arms was growing longer and thicker, Elena realized, turning to white fur again. His shoulders hunched and his jaw lengthened.

Zander wasn't changing fully this time, she saw, but he was somewhere between a wolf and a man now. Roy and Alex glanced anxiously at each other, but no one moved.

Finally, Zander's captive seemed to give up and grew still, his head hanging down against Zander's shoulder. His aura had calmed, Elena saw, its natural soft yellow color breaking through in patches.

Then Zander spoke, his voice half a growl, half human speech. "Why are you here?"

The guy was panting in time with Zander's breaths, and his answer seemed to be pulled out of him in gasps.

"To kill the girl," he said. "Kill everyone with her. Don't give up."

"Who told you to do this?" Zander asked. The guy panted against him, not answering, and Zander's voice dropped an octave, the growling note increasing. "Who was it?"

The guy thrashed once more and then went limp, supported only by Zander's arms around him, holding him up. "Didn't know him," he panted. "Some guy. He was tall." He licked his lips. "Yellow eyes like a coyote. He wanted us to meet him on the hills north of campus two nights from now. Midnight under the full moon. Bring the girl's head, or we'll suffer."

Elena caught her breath and looked at the others. Jack's eyes were wide, a smile beginning to play around the edges of his mouth, and Trinity was biting her lip. Stefan had grown very still and thoughtful.

Zander relaxed, shifting the guy's weight, and his captive went limp against him. "I don't think he has anything else to tell us," he said. "He smells like apples, though. They all do. Probably they work here at the orchard."

It took Elena a moment to catch his meaning, but then it dawned on her. "If the scent came from them, the orchard might have nothing to do with Solomon," she said.

Alaric cocked an eyebrow. "At least if they were compelled to break into your apartment to destroy the stave and kill your cat, it probably means Solomon can't come in without an invitation."

Elena shrugged. That wasn't very comforting, not if Solomon could send people in after her, and not if his magic could infiltrate her apartment. She thought of the ice cracking across her windows, and shivered.

"Would sending humans work? Could they kill you?" Meredith asked, looking at Elena. "They're human, but they've been Influenced. Surely that wouldn't count as not being supernatural."

Elena shrugged again. She didn't know, but she didn't really want to test the theory.

"It's irrelevant," Stefan said. His voice was sharp. "They'd never get to Elena."

"The important thing is that now we know where Solomon will be in two nights," Jack said softly.

Stefan smiled. "Maybe we can get the jump on him this time."

It wasn't much, not yet, but it was the first crack they'd found in Solomon's armor. It was a beginning.

12

Deep in Germany's Black Forest, Damon sank down onto the trunk of a fallen tree. Dampness seeped through the legs of his expensive jeans, now rumpled and smeared with mud.

"I hate this," he complained, dropping his head into his hands. He was dirty and exhausted and, most of all, hungry. Thick, dark conifers rose around them, their heavy branches blocking out the sky.

Leaning against a nearby tree, Katherine glanced wearily at him without answering. Her light blond hair, usually smooth and perfect, was a tangled mess, and there was dirt on her face. Still, she was in better shape than Damon, he thought bitterly. At least she had been able to Influence people to let her feed.

They'd been fleeing across Europe for days, losing themselves in countless city crowds. Budapest, Paris,

Berlin. But wherever they went, the packs of vampires had found them.

"We can't keep running," Damon said. "Maybe it's time we make a stand, choose a spot we can defend and take out as many of them as we can. We need to figure out who's behind this."

Katherine shook her head. "I don't know about you, but dying twice was enough for me. It's smarter to keep moving. We'll lose them eventually."

Damon felt a red wall of rage rising up in his mind. He was too old, too experienced, to be herded around like an animal, running from place to place in fear. Whoever was doing this, he wanted to rip them apart, feel their blood and flesh rend in his hands and between his teeth. "It would make me feel better if I killed someone," he muttered.

"Heavens." Katherine's tone was mocking. "Are you starting to regret the deal you made for little Elena? How does it go? You can't feed unless you romance them first?"

"Stop it," Damon said, suddenly feeling more tired than angry. "I'll kill whoever's behind this, that I promise you. The deal doesn't apply to vampires."

"Poor Damon," Katherine said, a new, softer tone in her voice. When Damon looked up, she was standing right in front of him, looking at him with clear blue eyes—a shade lighter than Elena's, his mind automatically categorized, but not really so different. She raised her wrist to her own mouth and bit down, opening her vein, and the forest was flooded with the rich scent of her blood. "Here, drink," she said, holding her arm out to him. Damon stared at her, and her mouth tightened in annoyance. "You can't keep going without anything to eat," she snapped. "You're a liability like this."

"Well, I'd hate to be a burden," Damon said with a shrug, taking her wrist and bringing it to his lips.

He hadn't tasted Katherine's blood since she first made him a vampire, and he was unprepared for the rush of memories it brought back to him. *A delicate girl, hardly more than a child, appearing at dusk in the rooms of his father's palazzo. Her hair was a fine light gold, shining in the candlelight as she sank into a low curtsy. Her skin was so pale that he could see the fine blue tracery of her veins when she reached out for him, and her lips were cool when he lowered his head to meet them.*

Damon's eyes were burning when he let go of Katherine's hand. Her pale pink lips parted in surprise, and he wondered if she, too, had just been transported back in time. His heartbeat quickened as he felt Katherine's blood running through him, warming him and bringing him strength. It wasn't as good as feeding on a human, but it would keep him going for a while.

"Thank you, darling," he said dryly.

Katherine's voice was light. "This whole situation should teach you not to make deals with Guardians. They're tricky, I hear."

Damon was opening his mouth to answer when a sound in the distance made him pause. He cocked his head to listen and heard it again: the crackle of footsteps on dry leaves, coming toward them, fast. "They've found us," he hissed.

He pulled his Power around him quickly, fiercely concentrating on the sensation of his own form dissolving and compacting. His bones thinned and reformed within him, changing shape, his fingers spreading into wings as his toes curled into claws. He had a moment to feel grateful for Katherine's blood: This was difficult to manage when he wasn't feeding regularly.

Then Damon, in the form of a crow, stretched his glossy black wings and rose past tree branches into the sky. He could feel the currents of air behind him shifting as Katherine took silent flight in the shape of a snowy owl.

They had escaped their enemies once more, for now. But Damon knew they couldn't keep going forever. Sooner or later, they would have to fight.

#TVD11KatherinetheTease

* * *

It was a warm, clear night. An almost-full moon shone overhead, and the scent of night-blooming jasmine rose up to Stefan on the balcony outside their apartment.

But Stefan wasn't here to appreciate the beauty of the evening. He sent out tendrils of his Power, questing, trying to sense whatever was out there. Why was he so *weak*?

Maybe Damon was right; maybe it was worth drinking human blood regularly for the strength it would give him. Stefan drank Elena's blood sometimes, and she drank his, but it was an act of love, not a feeding. He didn't take enough to make him strong. He swiped his hand across his face, irritated with himself, and tried to focus.

He couldn't sense anything. There was an Old One after Elena, who knew the loophole in her immortality and was sending humans after her. Stefan gripped the edge of the balcony and felt the metal begin to buckle beneath his hand. Conscientiously, he forced his fingers to relax. They didn't want to lose their security deposit.

Was that a footstep below, too light for human ears to hear? He froze, listening. The night was alive with a thousand sounds: insects buzzing, the soft beats of a bat's wings, the distant sound of traffic.

Again, almost right below, a footstep on the grass. Without stopping to think, Stefan launched himself over the rail, his canines lengthening as he leaped.

The warm, solid body beneath him let out a huff of surprise as he hit it, both of them slamming down on the ground. *Human*, he automatically classified, even as he reached for the throat.

It didn't matter. Human or not, he had to keep this person from Elena. But the realization slowed him a little, long enough for the figure underneath him to twist and kick hard at Stefan's chest. Stefan slammed him back onto the ground, baring his fangs—and then realized the person beneath him was Jack. For an instant, he didn't think he could stop. He didn't want to stop. Jack's heart was pounding, and Stefan's canines were sharp with anticipation. It would be easy.

He let go and rolled to one side. Jack lay flat on the ground, panting, one hand pressed against his chest.

"You're heavy," he said finally.

"I'm sorry." Stefan climbed to his feet and offered Jack a hand up. "I didn't realize it was you. I've been a little tense lately."

He could still hear Jack's heart beating, hard and fast, as he rose. Stefan averted his eyes from the vein at the side of Jack's neck, ignoring the thought of the rich blood rushing quickly beneath the skin. He needed to go out to the woods and feed properly, but guarding Elena was more important.

Jack brushed off his pants, which were covered with dirt. "Didn't mean to startle you. I'm just patrolling, keeping an eye out."

"I attacked too quickly," Stefan said, guilt slamming heavily into him. "I should have made sure of who you were before I jumped on you."

"Hey, don't worry about it." Jack waved a dismissive hand, although Stefan noticed he winced as he cautiously rolled his neck, checking to see if he was injured. "Guarding Elena is the important thing. Plus, I could totally take you down if I had to."

Stefan smiled dutifully at the joke, then stared out into the darkness, watching and listening. Far off, a car started up and drove in the opposite direction. There was no one else nearby that he could sense. "He's all I can think about," he said. "Solomon, I mean." Jack nodded, and Stefan went on. "We'd gotten to where the Old Ones weren't coming after Elena anymore. I was hunting them instead. I thought all this was over."

His hands curled into fists, and he felt his canines press sharp against his lips again, ready to bite. "We don't know where he is, and he's coming after Elena. I want to rip out his throat." Stefan glanced at Jack, feeling oddly ashamed at the admission.

Jack patted Stefan lightly on the shoulder. "This is normal, Stefan," he said reassuringly. "You feel this way because you're a warrior. Even though you're a vampire, you're a hunter, too. That means you're always prepared for a fight. And you have something worth fighting to protect."

Stefan looked up at the darkened windows of their apartment. Extending his Power, he could feel Elena sleeping deeply, her dreams troubled, but her breathing even. Jack was right, he thought. Elena was Stefan's to protect. She was worth fighting for.

"So the patient came in complaining of chest pains, but when we hooked him up to the EKG, he told us he'd changed his mind and that the pain was in his legs." Jasmine came out of her bedroom, holding a long golden necklace around her neck. "Can you fasten this for me?"

"Uh-huh," Matt said, looking out the window at the darkening sky. He had promised to meet Elena and the others at Dalcrest at nine, so they could canvass the hills around campus before midnight, when Solomon would show to meet the humans he'd influenced.

Matt knew he should leave, but he liked it here. Jasmine's apartment was warm, filled with texture and color: handmade bowls in the kitchen, red-painted walls with heavy woven hangings in the living room, a velvety sofa. A cozy nest, far from violence and vampires and hunters.

"Matt?" Jasmine said, and the part of Matt's mind that wasn't already out the door registered that she'd said something a moment before.

"What?" he asked. Jasmine arched her brows meaningfully and wiggled the necklace a little. "Oh." Matt moved her heavy fall of hair out of the way so he could work the catch. Her skin was honey golden and very smooth, and she smelled sweet. He stroked the back of her neck, once, twice, watching the tendrils of hair fall back into place around his fingers. "Why are you getting dressed up?"

Jasmine frowned. "Because we're going out." At Matt's blank look, she rolled her eyes. "Honestly, where is your mind today? I swear, you haven't heard a thing I've said in the last hour."

Matt could feel his cheeks flushing, his ears getting hot. She was right; he hadn't been listening. "I'm really sorry," he said awkwardly. "I promised to meet Elena and Stefan tonight."

"That's okay," Jasmine said, shrugging. "I'd have liked to have you to myself, but I haven't seen them in ages." Looking at Matt's expression, her face fell and she added hesitantly. "If that's all right?"

"I'm sorry," Matt said. Her mouth trembled, and he hastened to add, "It's just, there's some stuff going on with them. They wanted to talk to me alone about it. Just this time."

"Oh." Jasmine wrapped a finger in her long curls, tugging them straight. Her mouth was still soft and hurt. "Okay, well, call me tomorrow." She said it breezily, but Matt could tell she was upset. She knew he was lying, he realized.

"I'll see you later," Matt said, his stomach tying itself in knots. He hesitated in the doorway. There was a cool wind blowing, and the full moon shone, heavy in the sky. He wanted to stay, wanted just to wrap himself up in her, in her honey skin and soft smile. Jasmine tilted her face up toward him and he kissed her gently.

"I'll call you tomorrow," he said, his heart aching just a little bit.

And then he was on his way out into the night, shutting the door behind him.

* * *

"This customer's voice mailbox is full. Please try again later. Thank you," an electronic voice chirped. Elena pushed her phone's off button a little more violently than necessary.

Why hadn't Damon listened to any of her messages? He must have ignored every single one for his entire mailbox to be full.

"I'm worried about Damon," she told Stefan through the balcony doorway. He was pacing back and forth across the balcony, scowling at the tops of trees as if he could see straight through them to find someone lurking below.

"Damon's fine," he said absently.

"I don't think so," Elena said. "He's worried about something. I think he might be in danger."

Whenever she reached out to Damon through their shared connection, all she felt was a sort of grim anxiety. She closed her eyes and concentrated on their bond, but she couldn't get any clear picture, just images of forests and cities. It felt like he was running from something.

"If Bonnie were here, she could use a spell to contact him," she said, frustrated. "I wish . . . I can't *do* anything."

Stefan finally looked up to meet Elena's gaze. His face softened, and he took the few steps across the balcony to stand before her. "Elena," he said, reaching out to touch her cheek. "Just because Damon isn't responding to you doesn't mean something's wrong. He's always been hard to pin down. He'll get in touch in his own time."

Elena shook her head. "This time is different. I'm worried," she said.

Tilting her chin up, Stefan gazed into Elena's eyes. "I know," he said. "But with everything going on here, Damon's probably safest of all of us. And even if he *is* in trouble, Damon's very, very good at taking care of himself. I wish he were here, too, but only because he could help protect you from Solomon."

"I'm not helpless, Stefan," Elena said sharply.

Stefan blinked in surprise at her tone. "I never said you were," he replied. "But you're the one Solomon's after. Don't worry about Damon; worry about yourself."

"Okay," Elena said, sighing inwardly. She knew Stefan was only trying to protect her. But she'd saved people, she'd killed Klaus; surely she could hold her own against any threat.

She tried her best to push away her anxiety over Damon. Whatever was going on with him, she couldn't do anything to help him now. No matter how strongly she felt that something was *wrong*.

* * *

Elena's sensation of wrongness didn't go away, not even later, when they met the others on the hills overlooking campus. It was a clear night, the full moon high. Zander and his Pack were in wolf form and alert, sniffing the wind, their ears cocked for any sound. One of them, Daniel, raced around the others to greet them, his heavy tail wagging, and Zander snapped at him, herding him back into place.

Once upon a time, Elena remembered, she hadn't been able to tell any of the wolves apart—except for Zander, with his snow-white fur. Now they were as distinct to her in wolf form as they were as humans. The reddish-tinged one that was Shay yelped a short bark at oversize Jared. He pulled his lips back in a lazy laugh, cocking his black-tipped ears. Tristan sprang at Enrique, growling playfully, and toppled him to the ground, where they rolled in a mock battle. Zander yipped once and they sprang apart guiltily, joining the rest of their group as the Pack paced the hillside.

There were a couple of hours yet till midnight. If they could just figure out where Solomon would come from, they could get into position, launch an attack.

Elena shut her eyes and focused her Power, trying to force open the doors within herself that would help her track down evil. Nothing. With a huff of irritation, she opened her eyes again.

Matt was climbing up the hill toward Elena and Stefan. He carried a flashlight, which he cast over the trees and grass around them, but he didn't speak. He looked grim, his lips pressed tightly together.

Meredith and Alaric followed him, Alaric also holding a flashlight, while Meredith balanced her stave in one hand.

"Where do you think we should look?" Stefan asked, glancing at Meredith.

"If I were going to meet a bunch of brainwashed humans to get a report on their evil mission," Meredith said thoughtfully, "I'd head for a good, clear space with plenty of moonlight. He'll need light to see them, to Influence them. We could get into the tree cover near the biggest clearing and wait."

Stefan nodded. "Makes sense. The most open spot is up on top of the ridge. When Jack's team gets here, we'll head up."

Zander raised his head, his tail wagging, and a moment later, Jack and his group appeared over the crest of the hill. Jack and Roy raised their hands briefly, acknowledging Elena and the others, while Trinity shot Elena a warm smile. Darlene and Alex had their heads down, watching their step. Both carried heavy-looking bags of weapons.

"Looks like it's going to rain," Jack said in greeting when they reached them. Elena glanced up in surprise. It was true—black clouds had blocked out the moon while they talked, and the sky, clear a few moments ago, looked ominously heavy.

"That was fast," Alaric said uneasily. A cold wind blew across the hillside, lifting Elena's hair and bringing goose bumps out on her arms.

Meredith and Elena exchanged a worried glance. "Remember how Klaus could change the weather?" Elena said slowly. "Even Damon can make it storm, if he's angry enough."

Meredith swore. "Solomon knows we're here. He planned it."

"It's a trap. We need to get out of here." Stefan stepped closer to Elena, wrapping his arm around her shoulders protectively, his eyes scanning the tree cover around them.

Her heart sped up. Which way could they go to escape? The dark shadows beneath the trees were suddenly menacing.

Something hit Elena's cheek, and she jumped. At almost the same moment, one of the wolves yelped. Her arm stung, hit by something sharp and heavy.

"Hail!" Alex shouted just as a burst of lightning cracked across the sky. Thunder rumbled, and the wind picked up, whipping stinging shards of hail into their faces.

Stefan was trying to shout something above the roar of the wind, and Elena huddled closer to him, shielding her head from the hail. "What?" she yelled back.

"Let's go!" he shouted. The hail was coming down faster now, ripping into the ground. Stefan swung Elena into his arms and began to run at top vampire speed for the cover of the trees, wolves and hunters on his tail. Elena peered over Stefan's shoulder to see Matt and Alaric bringing up the rear, their flashlight beams swinging wildly.

There was a flash of bright light all around them and thunder cracked again, closer this time. Stefan backpedaled, Meredith and Jack flinching back just as a tree fell in flames right in front of them. Elena felt the searing heat of the flames on her cheeks, close enough that her hair sizzled. Behind them, another deafening crash resounded as lightning hit and flames rose up, blocking their retreat.

They were all trapped.

Stefan's arms tightened around Elena. Bright ashes were blowing everywhere, setting the grass around them ablaze. She blinked the smoke out of her eyes and tried to see.

Trinity was shouting something, but Elena couldn't hear her over the crackle of the flames. With a grimace, the brown-haired girl pulled some sort of long scythe from the case on her shoulder. As they watched, she began to gouge the ground, tearing up a long strip of sod.

Meredith stared at her for a second, and then began to imitate her, using the sharp edges at the end of her stave to dig a trench.

They're getting rid of the grass so the fire can't get any closer, Elena realized. She struggled out of Stefan's arms and began to pull and yank at the grass as the rest of the hunters lowered their weapons to dig at the ground, making a firebreak. The wolves whined anxiously around them and one—Tristan, Elena thought, squinting through the smoke—gave a low, unhappy howl. She bent her head back down, pulling at the grass.

Hot ash scorched their skin, but soon they had carved out a fireproofed circle of black dirt around them. They stood in a tight group at the center of the firebreak, the wolves on the outer rim, growling at the flames as if they could scare them into submission. A spark flew to land on Meredith's cheek, and she batted it off, wincing with pain. *This isn't going to work,* Elena realized, her heart sinking.

They were still trapped, and Solomon's Power seemed limitless.

But as if the fire were losing interest in them, the flames began to die down, and the storm faded. "He's playing games," she told Stefan, as soon as the smoke had cleared enough for her to speak. "He could have killed us, but he's not trying, not yet. He wants us to be afraid of him."

"I know," Stefan said tightly. He looked down at her, his mouth a narrow line and his green eyes dark with worry. "I'm afraid of what's going to happen when he does try."

"I'm the one he wants," Elena said miserably. "You're all in danger because of me."

Dark steam was still rising from the ground around them. The stench of burning was everywhere.

But the fire was out, and the clouds were clearing. Looking up, Elena saw that the moon shone peacefully overhead once more. If not for the damage that had been done to her friends— Jared's fur was ragged and scorched, burned right off in a couple of places, and a long red burn was rising on Darlene's cheek—she could almost believe she'd imagined the whole thing.

Matt coughed, a deep, rattling cough, and waved the smoke away.

"We know he's *somewhere*," Jack exclaimed, his face smudged with soot. "He's in the area. Even he doesn't have enough Power to do this from too far away. It's the best lead we've ever had, because he's not going to leave—" He broke off.

"Until I'm dead," Elena finished, her voice flat.

Jack winced, looking apologetic.

"We will not use Elena as bait," Stefan said coldly. "Our first priority is keeping her safe."

"But I won't be safe until we find Solomon," Elena told him, guilt stabbing through her chest. Everyone was risking their lives for her, and so far she hadn't been able to do anything to help, despite all her Power. "Look, I haven't been much use in tracking him. I think we should call in Andrés. Maybe he can help."

Just thinking of Andrés made Elena feel better. He'd taught her how to access and control her Power, but more than that, he was her friend. Andrés was wise. He understood Elena, and his Guardian Power, while different from her own, was equally strong.

"We can do this," she told the others, looking at the dying flames all around them. "We're not going to give up until we find Solomon, and kill him."

#TVD11LightningStrikes

The flames burned fiercely, yellow and orange with a flash of cold azure at the base. Frowning with concentration, Bonnie refused to be pulled into their hypnotic patterns. She clutched her falcon charm tight in one hand and breathed deeply, calling upon the stone's properties.

The charm Damon had given her was made of blue lace agate, which contained the properties of tranquility, and balance between mind, body, and spirit. This balance allowed Bonnie to access more Power than she'd ever dreamed of.

The falcon was cool in her palm, the sharp points of its beak and claws almost painful as she clutched it, yet somehow the little sharp pricks were reassuring. Bonnie could feel her own energy flowing into the stone and then circling back to her, calmer and steadier. After a few moments, she turned this Power outward to the flames, as easily as flipping a switch.

The flames flickered once and then went out.

Bonnie's new friends burst into applause and came up to congratulate her. Poppy squeezed her shoulders in a side hug, while Rick thumped her enthusiastically on the back. Marilise, always more reticent, hung back, but the smile on her face was one of pure delight. Bonnie smiled back at her proudly.

"Bonnie, that was amazing!" Alysia was grinning so widely that her freckles flowed together in little islands of brown across her cheeks. "I can't believe how far you've come in such a short time!"

Bonnie really couldn't believe it either. Finding her working stone had been a big step. The fact that it had come from the necklace Damon had sent her for her birthday couldn't be a coincidence. Sometimes he *knew* things about her; she was sure of it.

During the short time she had been with this group, she'd learned so much. Rick had turned out to know more about astrology and the influence of the stars and planets than anyone Bonnie had ever met. Marilise grew her own herbs at her cottage in North Carolina and had, in her gentle, quiet way, shown Bonnie helpful new ways of using them. And Poppy could see the future in crystal balls and cards—with more control than Bonnie had ever had over her own visions.

Tonight they, and all the other groups, had gotten a chance to demonstrate their new skills to everyone else.

Now Bonnie, full of gratitude, pulled Alysia into a spontaneous hug. "Thank you," she said. "If you hadn't talked me into coming here, I never could have done that. Every day, I can feel myself getting stronger and stronger."

Alysia's grin spread even wider, and she squeezed Bonnie back affectionately. "I'm glad you're here. You're making me look good." She stuck out her tongue playfully at an older man on the other side of the room, and he threw back his head and laughed. There was a core group of five who had organized the retreat, and each was in charge of mentoring a group of recruits. Alysia had said there was a friendly rivalry among the core group as to whose protégés would learn the most.

Bonnie glanced around the massive apartment, which had seemed so frightening at first but was now almost cozy, full of magic. It took up three floors of the building, complete with balconies and a roof deck. It felt like an expensive, grown-up version of a college dorm, Bonnie thought, communal and built for temporary living rather than someone's home.

"And now for the feast!" Alysia exclaimed, leading Bonnie to the dining room as the others followed. "It's a celebration," she explained. "So we threw together something special."

A wall of windows covered one wall of the dining room, looking out over the car headlights tracing a river of light far below. Alysia had created one of her beautiful illusions—pale flower petals falling ceaselessly from the ceiling, disappearing before they hit the floor.

The long table in the center of the room was heaped with food: a hodgepodge of everyone's favorites, from roast chicken to curry to peanut brittle to a bright pile of stir-fried vegetables. "Yum," Bonnie said and took a seat. "It's like a magic menu."

"I wish," Alysia said, rolling her eyes. "We were working on this all afternoon."

Bonnie was reaching for a platter of pork chops when her phone rang. *Zander*. "Oh, I need to take this. I'll be right back," she said, excusing herself and slipping out of the dining room.

"Hey," she answered, once she was alone back in the mosaic-floored living room where she had first met her team. "How's it going? I miss you."

"Sure you do." Zander's voice sounded rougher than usual, tired, but she could hear the smile in it. "That's because I'm *awesome*."

"Modest, too," Bonnie told him. She wandered over to a window and looked out at the streets far below. "How are things there?" Zander didn't say anything for a moment, and Bonnie tensed. "What's going on?"

"I'm thinking," Zander said. "How's witch camp?"

"Witch camp is fantastic. Soon I will be the queen of all witches. Seriously, I'm getting really strong." She wanted to go into more detail, tell Zander all the amazing things she was learning to do, but she didn't like the way he had paused when she asked him what was going on back home. His voice wasn't quite right—he sounded worried. She used her firmest tone. "What do you mean you're *thinking*? Give me a straight answer. Is everything okay?"

Zander sighed. "The Old One—Solomon—is getting closer. He's sent compelled humans after us. And he killed Elena's cat. Last night, we thought we had him, but we just stumbled into a trap." He paused. "He drew lighting and fire down around us."

Bonnie stiffened, feeling the blood drain out of her cheeks. Fire was one thing that the Pack *couldn't* fight. "I'm coming home," she said.

"No."

"You need me." She was already crossing the living room, heading for the stairs that would lead to her bedroom. She could pack and be at the airport in an hour, catch the next flight to Richmond or Washington, D.C. . . . "You'll pick me up at the airport, right?"

"Bonnie, stop," Zander insisted. "Listen to me."

"I have to be there!"

"We can handle it!" Zander said loudly, and Bonnie stopped in her tracks.

"If you're in danger—"

"We've got the Pack," Zander interrupted. "We've got hunters; we've got Stefan. We've got Elena, and she's bringing her other Guardian friend out. Solomon's tough, but there's a whole superhero alliance here."

Bonnie felt like her heart was being squeezed. "You don't need me?" she said in a tiny voice.

"Of course we need you," Zander said, his voice warm and reassuring. "*I* need you. Even when you're not here, you're helping protect us. We're all using the charms and everything you left. But right now, you need to stay there, keep working on your own stuff. You'll be stronger than ever when you come back, and then you'll fix whatever we haven't taken care of yet. Trust me and the Pack and the others for now, okay?"

Wavering, Bonnie closed her eyes for a moment. Her friends were in danger.

But it was true that she needed to be stronger if she was really going to be useful. The agate falcon rested cool against her collarbone—it never seemed to get warm—and she tried to take comfort in its calming properties.

"Trust us," Zander said again. "We want you back, but not till you're ready. Believe me, I miss you like crazy, but it'll all be okay. We'll hold down the fort."

"Okay." Bonnie bit her lip. "I'm going to learn everything that might help us, and then I'm on the first plane back."

I hope I'm doing the right thing, she thought.

tefan stared at the row of small white bottles on the drugstore shelf and looked at Elena's list again. *Moisturizer,* he read. It seemed like that ought to be simple, but there were fifteen different brands lined up in front of him, divided into different categories: *revitalizing,* he read, and *tone correcting,* and *age defying.*

Age defying? Stefan shook his head. Elena was going to look eighteen forever; surely that wasn't the one she wanted.

His phone buzzed, and he pulled it out of his pocket, hoping it wasn't Elena with more additions to the shopping list.

Damon, said the display.

A bubble of relief rose up in Stefan's chest. He'd been positive that Damon was fine and would get back in touch when he was ready, and he'd been right. But it was nice to have it confirmed.

"Elena's been worried about you," Stefan said in greeting when he answered the phone.

"I guess the Guardians' bond is still good, then. Nice to know they do quality work," Damon answered. His voice sounded tired, rougher than Stefan was used to hearing it, and very far away.

"Damon?" Stefan asked, gripping the phone. "Are you okay? Where are you?"

There was a shifting, as if Damon was looking around. "Let's see," he said. "Casinos. Sunshine. Yachts. Monaco. Not for long, though, I'm afraid."

"What's going on?" Stefan asked, grabbing a bottle of moisturizer at random and tossing it into his basket. There was a long silence on the other end of the line, and he shifted the phone to his other ear. "Are you there?"

Damon sighed. "There's something after Katherine and me," he said, sounding a little embarrassed. "Wherever we go, packs of vampires come after us. I wanted to know if you had any idea who they are or what's going on. They're strong, and there are a lot of them. It's nothing we can't handle," Damon added quickly. "But it's getting tiresome."

"That sounds strange," Stefan began, worried, and then something Damon had said finally clicked. "Wait—you're traveling with *Katherine*?" he asked sharply. "Is she hunting for you?" *Trust Damon to find a way around the rules the Guardians gave him*, he thought. And Katherine, of all people: After everything she'd done, how could Damon trust her?

"You think I'm cheating?" Damon asked, his voice flattening dangerously. "You should know better than anyone, I always keep my word." There was a long pause, and Stefan kneaded the bridge of his nose between two fingers, feeling guilty. He always assumed the worst of Damon, but that wasn't fair.

Damon sighed again, wearily. "I didn't call to fight, little brother," he said. "I just want to know if you have any idea what's going on."

"Right. Sorry. I don't want to fight either. I know you're not hunting," Stefan apologized. It was true: Damon wouldn't take an unwilling victim, not with Elena so linked to him that she'd be able to tell. "Well, I don't know if this is related, but there's another Old One here in town. Solomon. And he's after Elena."

"After Elena?" Damon's voice got sharper, focused. A woman said something behind him—*Katherine*, Stefan realized—and he replied, his voice muffled, then came back on the line. "Is Elena in danger?"

"It'll be okay. I've hunted a lot of Old Ones since you left. And you know how strong Elena is," Stefan said. There was no point in making Damon worry; he couldn't do anything more than the rest of them could. Which seemed to be nothing at this point. "Andrés just got here to help us track Solomon down."

"And then bing, boom, you'll take him out," Damon said lightly. "Nice to know you've got things under control. I don't see how this could be related, though. The vampires coming after us aren't Old Ones. If anything, they feel . . . new."

"New like newly made?" Stefan said. "You should be able to handle them easily, then."

Damon laughed a short, dry laugh. "You'd think so," he said. "No, it's not that they feel newly made, exactly, they're just . . . *different*, I suppose."

"You're not making a lot of sense, Damon," Stefan told him. The drugstore was almost empty, but the elderly cashier was peering at him from the other end of the aisle, her eyebrows raised. Stefan turned away from her, hunching his shoulders. He needed to keep his voice down. That was the problem with small towns: Someone was always watching you.

"When you've dealt with your little problem there, why don't you come out here?" Damon said. There was an artificial lightness to his voice as he added, "Come on, Stefan. It'll be fun. A little gambling, a little sailing, a little vampire killing. When was the last time you were in Monaco?"

"I can't," Stefan said automatically. "I need to be here to protect Elena."

There was another long pause, and Damon said, grimly, "I thought you said she was fine."

"She is, but . . ." Stefan could hear his own voice rising in irritation, and he stopped himself. Damon was his brother, and he'd saved Stefan's life more than once.

And he knew that, if Damon suspected how bad things were, he would come rushing back to fight on their side. He was better off out of it.

"I'm sorry," Stefan said, his voice gentle. "Elena will be fine. And I know you and Katherine will survive. You always do."

"I hope so," Damon said. "But it sounds like you've made your choice, anyway." The line went dead. Stefan stared down at the phone in his hand for a moment, wondering if he should call Damon back. The cashier down at the end of the store was still watching him. He tucked the phone back into his pocket.

Damon's tone had been bitter at the end, and Stefan felt bad about it, he really did. His brother had called to ask him for help, something he rarely did, and Stefan had turned him down. Guilt ran sharp through his veins. He couldn't worry about Damon, he reminded himself. Damon would be fine. It was Elena who mattered.

* * *

"Marisol's amazing," Andrés said happily. "We've been doing research in the rain forest, classifying plants no one knew about before, and we both love it. The life force there is so wonderful; even though she's not a Guardian, I think she feels it as much as I do."

Elena watched Andrés's smile light up his face, his warm brown eyes shine. She remembered how much sorrow he'd carried with him when they first met, after the death of the man who'd raised him. It was good to see the joy shining through him now.

"I'm so happy for you," she said, squeezing her friend's hand. "Have you told her you're a Guardian?"

"Of course." Andrés sounded surprised. "How could we love each other if she didn't know the truth about me?"

Elena thought of Matt's insistence on keeping the supernatural hidden from Jasmine, and shook her head. "I don't think you could, not forever," she agreed, feeling a pang of sorrow for Matt.

Stefan's key rattled in the lock, and Elena and Andrés looked up, smiling in welcome. Stefan smiled back automatically, his eyes searching out Elena's as they always did. As he leaned over to kiss her hello, Elena noticed tight lines of tension around his mouth.

"Did something happen?" she asked.

"I talked to Damon," Stefan told her.

"You did?" Relief flooded through Elena, mixed with a slightly miffed feeling: Damon had called Stefan, but not her? After all the messages she had left him? "Is he okay? Where is he?"

"He's fine," Stefan said. "He's in Monaco."

Monaco. Glamorous, full of life. Sounded like Damon. But then, why the angry, anxious emotions that had streamed—were *still* streaming—through the connection between them? "Did he get my messages?" she asked hesitantly. "And the e-mails?"

"He didn't say," Stefan told her. "We didn't talk for very long."

Elena frowned. "Well, why—" But Stefan was avoiding her eyes, his face closed off tightly. There was something he didn't want to tell her. Elena bit her lip. Maybe she should let it rest for now. "I'm glad he's all right, anyway," she said. "And wait till you hear what we figured out."

Andrés cleared his throat and broke into a grin, his eyes sparkling with excitement. "We were talking over the situation," he said, "and I thought of something that may help. Once, back when I first came into my Powers, I needed to trace an animal spirit who had been making trouble in town. The problem was, no one knew who the spirit was: She could have taken any kind of human disguise. My mentor, Javier, and I worked together and I learned how to do, er . . ." He waved his hand impatiently, looking for the words. "I guess you'd call it a vision spell? I was able to channel my Power through something we knew the spirit had seen in the past and find my way back to what she was seeing in the present."

"I'm not sure I understand," Stefan said.

Elena bounced on her heels, tugging at his sleeve in her excitement. "If we find something that we know Solomon has looked at, Andrés might be able to see what Solomon's looking at *now*!" she exclaimed. "We could figure out where he's hiding!"

"But we don't know what he's seen," Stefan said, frowning. "The things that happened here, with Sammy and my stave, he must have compelled humans to do."

"The ice?" Elena wondered. "He wasn't there, but he must have seen it somehow, right? Could we use the windows, or the bed . . . ?"

Andrés was shaking his head. "I think it has to be something more specific," he said. "Something Solomon actually laid eyes on, rather than controlling from a distance. And something recent, so a lot of people haven't seen it since he did. Too many people have been in and out of this apartment since then."

There was a baffled silence as they all thought.

"The car accident," Stefan said suddenly. Andrés and Elena stared at him, and then Elena began to smile.

"Of course," she said. "He would have watched, wouldn't he? That open road, surrounded by tree cover. It would have been easy for him." She got up and disappeared into the bedroom. "I haven't worn this shirt since that day," she said, coming out with a white shirt in one hand. "I washed out as much of the blood as I could, but it still needs to be dry-cleaned."

Andrés took it from her, turning the soft fabric over in his hands. "I'll try," he said. "Help me. The more Power we can put into this, the better." Elena took his hand and they both closed their eyes. For several moments, the only sound in the room was their breathing, deep and slow and in time with each other. Stefan held perfectly still.

Elena's blue eyes and Andrés's brown ones flew open at the same moment.

"Shining metal," Andrés said. "A young girl, fighting a tall dark-haired man. No, they're working out, very formal movements. A big open room."

"That's what Jack's seeing, not Solomon," Elena said instantly. "Jack saw me in that shirt, too. He must be training with his team."

"Okay, yes." Andrés's eyes were tracking back and forth rapidly, but Elena was sure he wasn't seeing the room they were in. "A library. Wooden tables, books. Oh, this one feels familiar. Meredith." He swallowed and tried again, his eyes moving faster. "Oh! I'm seeing through Stefan's eyes now." His gaze focused for a moment, snapping out of the trance. "That was curious, seeing myself from outside."

"Try again," Elena said. "Push past the people you recognize if you can. I think, other than Jack, Solomon would be the only stranger."

"Okay." They closed their eyes and breathed together for a moment, then began again. This time Andrés didn't speak immediately, his eyes moving more slowly back and forth, as if he was looking hard for something. There was a silence.

Elena was frowning, still holding tightly to Andrés hand, but her gaze shifted to meet Stefan's. "The apple men," she said slowly. "The ones who attacked us. They said something about Solomon having yellow eyes."

The fact had gotten lost in everyone's excitement over the supposed clue to *where* Solomon was going to be, but that was a clue, too, wasn't it? The idea of yellow eyes teased at the back of her mind, reminding her of something, but she couldn't quite place it.

"Does knowing he has yellow eyes help, Andrés?" Stefan asked quietly.

Andrés didn't answer, but his eyes moved a little faster. When he spoke, he sounded breathless. "A big room," he said. "Wainscoting, paneling. I can see a formal garden through the windows." He frowned. "There's a woman. No, a mannequin. In a long dress, blue, with a full skirt. A large fireplace."

Stefan looked baffled. "An old mansion?" he asked doubtfully. "Something at the college, maybe?"

But Elena knew. "The Plantation Museum," she gasped. "Down near the river. It's got to be."

Spontaneously, she hugged Andrés, then jumped to her feet and hurled herself into Stefan's arms. "We can do it," she said, her voice muffled against his shoulder. "We've finally got him."

Stefan nodded and held her close for a second. His arms were strong around her, and, when he kissed her, soft and sweet, she felt a flash of how he wanted to protect her, hold her here forever safe in his arms.

Finally he let go and headed for the closet where they kept his weapons. "Call the others," he said. "We should attack tonight."

eredith felt as tense as the string of a bow, taut and ready to fire. "And I have a cross-bow," she muttered to herself, "so that's convenient."

The weapon was smooth and reassuringly heavy in her hand, and she had her hunter's stave strapped to her back. When she got close enough for the stave to be useful, she would drop the bow.

The sun was setting, its last long rays coloring the horizon. Meredith, Alaric, and Stefan were coming up on the east side of the Plantation Museum, concealed behind the remnants of what had once been slave cabins. Jack's team, Matt, and the Pack would be circling around the house, ready to approach from any angle.

Her earpiece crackled to life as Jack's voice said, "In position," and Trinity answered "In position."

"In position," Meredith repeated. Alaric glanced over as he pulled out a crossbow of his own and headed farther into the garden: As the least powerful fighters, he and Matt were supposed to stick to the long-range weapons, keeping their distance from Solomon and whoever was in the house with him. Andrés would hang back, too, wielding his Guardian Powers if he could.

Stefan slipped away from them around the side of the cabins. A minute later, his voice chimed in. "In position."

The earpieces belonged to Jack's team, another clever tool from their arsenal. Meredith couldn't believe she had never thought of using them before. It allowed them all—except for the Pack, who were in wolf form right now—to coordinate their attack from all over the museum and its grounds, fully aware of what everyone else was doing. And the Pack had their own forms of communication, could fight as a unit with no need for speech.

They were all here, and ready. Everyone but Elena. It felt weird to go into a fight without Elena, but Stefan had insisted: Solomon wanted Elena dead, and she would stay as far from him as possible. Elena had argued, but finally had agreed to go to the movies; Solomon wouldn't come after her in the middle of a crowded theater. Or so they all hoped.

Elena's lethal blood was with them, though. A thin coat, mixed with water, had been applied to the killing edge of every weapon they carried, and filled the tiny hypodermics in the ends of Meredith's special hunter's stave. Meredith only hoped there would be enough to do the job.

The sun sank below the horizon, and the dim security lamps around the museum snapped on. Meredith tested her bowstring and fitted an arrow carefully into place.

At first she'd instinctively objected to the idea of coming after a vampire at night. But the Plantation Museum was full of visitors and workers during the day, and none of them were willing to endanger innocent people if they could possibly help it.

Now Andrés just had to use his Power, strengthened by the life force of the plants in the garden, to sense if Solomon was still seeing the museum, and they could begin. Meredith's earpiece crackled again, and Andrés's voice came through, hushed and excited. "He's here. Solomon's inside the house. He's facing a wall, so I can't tell which floor he's on."

Meredith adjusted her grip on her crossbow and slipped forward. The night was silent, almost as if she were alone, but she knew that all around her the others were coming forward, tightening around Solomon's hiding place like a noose.

A shadowy figure crossed in front of the mansion—a guard, Meredith realized, and she glanced to her right.

One of the wolves was already skulking through the bushes toward the figure. He raised his head and looked back at her, cocking his ears forward in a prearranged signal. *A vampire, not a compelled human.*

Without hesitating, Meredith aimed the crossbow and fired. There was a soft thwack as the bolt found its mark. The vampire fell with a thud. Meredith hurried across the open lawn, staying low, the wolf keeping pace beside her.

She knelt to check the vampire and found the bolt had gone through his heart. The wolf—Daniel, she now realized—sniffed cautiously at the wound and then looked up at Meredith, giving her a single tail wag of approval.

"Guard down. Ready," she said softly, touching her earpiece. In a single movement, she dropped the crossbow, took her stave from its sheath. The others were heading through windows and side doors. Meredith rested her hand for a moment on the rough gray fur of Daniel's back for reassurance; then together they slipped through the museum's front entrance.

By the door stood a hoopskirted mannequin, its blank face framed by a full curled wig, meant to represent the lady of the house back in the old plantation days. It filled so much space that it took Meredith a moment to realize there was a person at the admissions desk behind it.

She hesitated for a second too long. The tall, elegant blonde behind the desk looked natural there, like any museum docent—except for the fangs that she bared at them. Another vampire of Solomon's. She started to lunge at Meredith, and Meredith ducked quickly, raising her stave, knowing she was too late, that her split second of delay would prove fatal.

Then there was a crash of shattering glass as, faster than any human could move, Stefan hurtled through the window, grabbing the woman and swinging her around. He snapped her neck in a single, clean motion. Meredith moved forward to stake the woman in the heart, her movements perfectly matched to Stefan's, as they always were.

"Thanks," she said, when she'd caught her breath. He nodded in response, turning toward the hall. Meredith turned with him, raising her stave in anticipation.

They could hear the others all over the mansion, glass shattering and the sound of blows. A wolf snarl came from a room farther down. Daniel tensed and slipped quietly past them, the fur on his shoulders bristling. Footsteps thudded down the stairs.

Stefan stood a little in front of her, his whole body tense and ready, his teeth bared. He held his machete easily in one hand. He looked like something primal and wild, Meredith thought fleetingly, like a warrior out of prehistory.

And then Solomon's minions burst through the door.

Meredith didn't think after that, just slid smoothly into battle, kicking and leaping and twisting as her hunter instincts commanded, her stave slicing through the air. A dark-haired vampire girl lunged for her throat, and Meredith stabbed her smoothly through the heart.

She was aware of Stefan working fluidly next to her, their blows and parries complementing each other's instinctively. They turned together, cutting the heads neatly off a pair of vampires. Blood geysered up from the vampires' throats, splattering the walls, and the bodies fell to the floor with a thud.

Then the room was empty, except for the four vampire corpses, lying on a floor slick with blood. Meredith and Stefan finally turned to look at each other, breathing heavily.

They could hear the sounds of the battle still going on throughout the lower floor of the mansion—a muffled cry, the angry clang of metal weapons colliding, the sharp barks of the Pack. Nodding at Stefan, Meredith raised her stave once more, and they went forward together into the fight.

They moved swiftly and silently through the museum. A vampire came toward Meredith and she sidestepped his blow, sweeping his feet out from under him with one kick. Before the vampire could hit the floor, Stefan had torn off his head.

It's like a dance, Meredith thought, half-dazed. Something about the smooth interplay between her and Stefan, the sweep of their weapons and the strikes of their limbs, worked like the best dancing couples. They didn't need to speak; she could sense his movements almost before they happened.

Three vampires raced across the hall in front of them, Darlene in hot pursuit as she pulled the trigger of her flamethrower. A jet of fire caught one of the vampires, and he gave a high, terrified scream as he burned.

Alex was halfway up the stairs, three vampires surrounding him, but he had a fierce grin on his face and an actual broadsword in his hand—even in the midst of battle, Meredith couldn't help being amazed by that—moving so quickly it was barely more than a blur of metal.

They passed a roped-off living room, where Tristan was tearing the throat out of a vampire, the fur of his muzzle matted with gore.

There was no sign of a vampire with yellow eyes.

At last, Meredith and Stefan came to a deserted dining room laid as if for a holiday feast. Silver and crystal sparkled, and a fake suckling pig, shiny with varnish, took pride of place on the table. This was the first room Meredith had come to where the walls were not spattered with blood, the hand-blocked wallpaper cleanly traced with Victorian vines and blossoms.

Stefan tensed, hearing a sound Meredith couldn't make out, and whipped around toward the door—but it was only

Jack and Trinity, blood-spattered though seemingly uninjured. Zander and Shay, wolf-formed, padded in through a door at the other end of the room. They were bloody, too, and Zander was limping, but their tails were high with triumph.

"We've been through the rooms upstairs, but we didn't find any sign of Solomon," Jack said, scrubbing a hand over his tired face and smearing more blood across his cheek. "I think we have to face that he's disappeared again. Even though Andrés thought he was here."

Trinity leaned back against the wall, her usually cheerful face glum. "Maybe it was a trick all along," she said. "He likes to tease us. Finding him like this seemed too easy."

Meredith's shoulders slumped. Had they really fought so hard, for nothing? Stefan was gripping the machete so tightly his knuckles were white with strain.

"No," he said, almost choking on his rage. "It's not acceptable. We have to end this."

"Maybe we do," a light, cultivated voice interrupted from the doorway. Meredith tried to turn, tried to raise her stave, but she suddenly found that she couldn't move.

Slow, deliberate footsteps crossed the floor behind her. The room had become very cold.

There was a rush of Power, and Zander slammed back against the wall, his paws scrabbling helplessly, long claws scraping against the floor. The Power flung Shay through the window, the glass shattering as her thick-furred body slammed through it.

As frost began to form in Meredith's hair, Solomon finally stepped into her field of vision. He was good-looking in a harsh way, tall, all lean muscles and graceful, purposeful movement, dressed simply in jeans and a shirt. Tawny hair fell to the nape of his neck, and his features were sharply cut. He could have passed for a human on the street.

He glanced at Meredith as he passed, and she slammed backward as if she'd been shoved, her head banging hard against the wall, her teeth jarring with the impact.

"Stefan." Solomon stopped to peer into the younger vampire's face. He sounded amused. "I thought you'd find me." He raised a hand and touched Stefan's face gently. Blood began to run from Stefan's nose, coating his chin and running down his neck. Solomon watched him for a few moments, then made a soft, discontented sound and turned away.

A moment later, he was gazing into Meredith's face. His eyes were almost golden, she saw, and bright with malice. "Meredith," Solomon said, as if he knew her. "I've been looking forward to meeting you." He watched her carefully, and she felt herself growing colder and colder. Something tightened inside her head with a sharp snap, and a hot stream ran down her face—blood, she realized, like Stefan. "Oh, no," he said, sighing, and made a wry face. "A pity." He moved on to Trinity and Jack, across the room. The painful tightness in Meredith's head eased a little but didn't end.

Trinity looked as if she'd been caught about to speak, her mouth partially open. She was as still as a mannequin. Beside her, the window was silvered with frost. Meredith was freezing.

"Jack!" Solomon peered delightedly into the hunter's face. "You've been looking for me for a long time, haven't you?" Meredith wondered what the Old One was doing, why he was toying with them. She was reminded of making rounds at her wedding reception: greeting everyone, making small talk.

She couldn't see Solomon's face, but she figured he was doing to Jack whatever it was he'd done to her and Stefan, expected to see Jack's face running with blood. Instead she heard Solomon chuckle, a sudden, surprised sound. "Oh," he said. "No, you won't do at all."

Solomon moved on again, and Meredith could see that Jack wasn't bleeding after all. There was a thin coating of frost on him, though, and his eyes looked furious.

"Hello, Trinity," Solomon said, and there was a new note in his voice, almost . . . thoughtful. His hand traced over Trinity's shoulder, long fingers running across her collarbone. "You're strong. And tall, I like tall. Maybe you're worth my time." The cold in the room intensified sharply, and Meredith felt as if her skin, unable to shiver, might crack like the glass of Elena's windows.

"Maybe," Solomon said again, sounding pleased. Meredith couldn't see what he was doing to Trinity—his body was blocking her view of his hands, but they were on Trinity's face. Then he stepped back and Meredith had a moment to feel relief: The girl was unchanged, her mouth still frozen in shock.

But as Meredith watched in horror, a thin tendril of blood began to run from Trinity's open mouth, tracing over her chin and onto the floor. A moment later, blood was running from her nose, dripping like tears from her eyes. So much blood, much more than had come from Stefan or Meredith. Solomon cocked his head, watching Trinity closely, his tongue running across his lips. Her hair matted as blood began to run from her ears.

"Pretty," Solomon said, his voice a warm purr. "I *like* this one."

No, no, no, Meredith thought frantically. *I have to do something!* The blood was freezing on Trinity's face, her nostrils caking with dark red ice. She was still motionless, but now there was the faintest choking noise coming from her. Solomon leaned forward, intent. *Help!* Meredith thought, still unable to move.

Near the window, something shifted.

Meredith stared as one of the vines in the wallpaper twisted, lengthening across the wall. Was she going crazy? Suddenly the wallpaper was writhing with vines, the flowers expanding as the tendrils reached the carpet and continued to spread.

And the room was getting warmer. The blood on Trinity's face was thawing and beginning to flow again.

Andrés, she thought. It must be Andrés. He had Power over life and growing things; this warmth and motion must come from him.

Solomon, focused on Trinity, didn't seem to notice the wallpaper. A single vine ran across the table, nudging the fake suckling pig with a scraping noise, and Meredith held her breath. Whatever was happening, they needed Solomon unaware.

Wait a second, she realized—she *held her breath*. However Solomon had frozen her in place, taken her power over her own body, his Influence was fading. Carefully, she flexed her muscles, and her fingers tightened slowly on her stave. She couldn't move her arms, not yet, but she blinked and shifted her gaze to Stefan. He had straightened and was glaring at Solomon, his whole body tensed.

A vine wrapped itself around Solomon's ankle. With a grunt, he pulled away, his concentration on Trinity broken.

Another, thicker vine whipped itself around his waist, and he snarled, tearing it off.

In that moment, Stefan struck. He leaped forward and swung his machete high overhead, its blade coated in Elena's blood, slamming it down to slice cleanly through Solomon's skull and torso.

For one moment, Solomon held together, a line of blood running straight down from his forehead to his waist. Then, with a sickening squelch, his body fell in two clean pieces onto the floor.

Everything was very quiet.

Solomon's control over her broke with a sudden snap. Shuddering, Meredith took a long, shaky gasp of air, and everything came back into focus.

Stefan was breathing hard, his eyes wide and dark, his canines extended. Meredith hurried to his side and began kicking the sections of Solomon's body apart, just in case he had some regenerative Power. "We did it," she started to say, "we—" But she broke off as Trinity collapsed behind her, her body shaking in sudden and terrifying convulsions.

Jack rushed to kneel beside his fellow hunter. "She's still bleeding," he said urgently, his hands moving carefully over her.

The doors at both ends of the dining room slammed open as the others started to spill in. "We were frozen in that parlor upstairs," Darlene explained, then gasped, seeing Trinity. "Oh my God!" She ran to kneel on the girl's other side. Alex and Roy followed, their faces shocked. Shay scrambled back through the window, girl formed again and swearing, her face and arms dotted with tiny cuts.

There was a pounding of boots in the hall, and Matt pushed his way through a crowd of werewolves, dangling a crossbow from one hand and pulling Andrés with the other. "Andrés did it," he announced. "He just pulled the life force out of that garden and sent it *racing* through here. The whole picture of what was going on was hanging before us like some kind of vision or something. I've never seen anything like it." Andrés nodded, looking drained but triumphant.

The smiles dropped off both their faces as they saw Trinity's body, now terribly still, lying surrounded by her friends. "Is she . . .?" Matt asked, a quaver in his voice.

Zander rose to his feet, changing from wolf to man in one motion. "We have to get her to a hospital," he said, nodding to his Pack. "Jared, Dan, find something you can use as a stretcher." The two nodded and began to rise, but Jack stepped forward, shaking his head firmly.

"Stop," he said. "We can't take her to a hospital like this. I don't think it'll help. Whatever Solomon did to her, they can't fix. And those are impossible injuries. There will be too many questions." He and Zander stared at each other, both steely with determination.

"We can't let her *die*," Roy protested, a note of desperation in his voice.

"No one's going to die," Stefan said quietly. There was blood running through his hair and spattered across his face from the death blow he'd dealt Solomon, but his voice was so full of authority that both Jack and Zander, each a leader in his own right, turned to listen. "We'll take her to my apartment." He swiftly bit at his wrist and held it to Trinity's slack mouth, rubbing her throat with his other hand to force the unconscious girl to swallow. "My blood will help for now. I just hope it's enough."

Zander and Jack both nodded. At the gesture, Daniel and Jared went and cleared the dining table, taking the cloth to put carefully under Trinity. The girl moaned in pain, her head turning restlessly from one side to the other as they tried to shift her, her eyes moving frantically beneath their lids. Meredith wasn't sure whether it was a good or bad sign that Trinity didn't wake up.

She made her way through the crowd of hunters and werewolves over to Matt and Andrés. "Are you okay?" she asked quietly. Matt was frowning, his gaze on Trinity but his eyes distant, as if he was thinking hard. Andrés leaned against him, looking shaky and disoriented.

"Yeah," Matt said, blinking. "Yeah, I'm fine. I have to go do something, though. Can you help Andrés? Using that much Power took a lot out of him. He can barely stand."

Carefully, he shifted Andrés's weight onto Meredith's shoulder.

The Guardian was heavier than she would have guessed. He was practically asleep, dead weight against her. Matt gave her a brief, distracted smile, then slid through the crowd and was gone.

"All right there, Andrés?" Meredith asked, nudging him into an easier position and slipping her arm around him. "What does Matt think he's doing, taking off *now*?"

She wasn't really expecting an answer, but Andrés smiled at her. "Matt has been wrestling with his conscience," he murmured. "He's between a rock and a hard place, as I think the expression goes . . ."

Meredith tightened her grip on him. "What do you mean?" But the Guardian only hmmed softly, his gaze foggy with exhaustion. His thick black lashes fluttered against the shadows beneath his eyes.

They were ready to move Trinity now, the werewolves carrying her carefully, Jack and Stefan keeping pace beside her makeshift stretcher. Jack was holding Trinity's hand. As they left, he cast a swift glance over the room. "Can you take care of this place?" he asked Darlene.

Meredith looked around the room at the floor coated with blood and gore, the windows shattered, Solomon's body in pieces, vampire corpses scattered through the hallways. Water was running in long dirty stains through the bloody wallpaper. Andrés's magic vines, wilting, ran across the floor. Even the suckling pig had smashed. There was no way they could leave the museum this way for innocent curators to find in the morning.

"What does he mean, take care of it?" she asked Darlene.

The older woman smiled grimly, the flamethrower hanging from her hand. "He means burn it to the ground," she said. "Want to help me find some gasoline?"

#TVD11SaveTrinity

rinity moaned and thrashed her head against the pillow, trying to pull away. Beneath her eyelids, her eyes moved rapidly. She was still trying to fight.

"You're safe now," Elena murmured, trying to soothe her. "We've got you." She stroked Trinity's hair carefully back from her forehead, and the girl stilled a little, whimpering. She was terribly pale. "It's taking her a long time to heal," Elena said nervously, looking up at Stefan.

"I know." Stefan ran his fingers unconsciously across the wrist he had fed Trinity from. "But giving her any more blood isn't safe. She'd rather die than be a vampire; any hunter would."

Elena's breath caught in her throat. Stefan thought that Trinity—funny, sweet-tempered Trinity, who had sparred with her and sympathized over Sammy's death—was dying. Elena didn't want to believe it, but Trinity looked so small and helpless lying there, trapped in her unconscious fight.

Jack nodded, his eyes fixed on his young teammate. His hair and clothes were spattered with blood and his face was exhausted, but he hadn't left Trinity's side. "All we can do now is watch over her," he said softly. "At least we killed Solomon."

Stefan nodded. "It was all thanks to Andrés," he said. "Without him, we never could have gotten free."

Andrés was slumped in a chair in the corner of the bedroom, completely asleep. Elena could sympathize. It sounded like he had channeled so much Power that he had burned himself out temporarily.

"Everyone fought hard," Meredith said with a brief smile, dried blood cracking on her face. "And we won."

Solomon was dead, Elena reminded herself. With all the worry over Trinity, she hadn't really let it sink in. It didn't feel like they'd won.

Glimpsing her own reflection in the window, she saw a pale, large-eyed girl, one who looked like the *victim* in a dark fairy tale, not the happy princess. She was edgy and anxious, as if there was some kind of doom hanging over her head. As if there was something terrible still out there in the dark.

Stefan had told Elena that Solomon was the same man who brushed past her outside the bar a while ago, with the yellow-green eyes. She shivered at the thought that he had touched her, and realized how close she could have been to death at that moment. *I'm being ridiculous*, she told herself. *Everything will be all right, as long as Trinity survives.*

Trinity shifted in the bed and gave a soft whimper, and Elena forced her attention back to the wounded girl.

The apartment was full, but it was very quiet, just the shuffle of feet in the hall as everyone—hunters, werewolves, Elena's friends—stopped by, one after another, to gaze in at Trinity as she struggled for life. They were all injured in varying degrees, with limps, bruises, and cuts, but no one was hurt as badly as Trinity. Her hair spread out over the pillow, and her lashes were dark against the pallor of her face. She was breathing slowly and shallowly. Elena realized that she was breathing in time with Trinity, trying to make her friend's breath get stronger by sheer force of will.

But there was one person she hadn't seen. "Where's Matt?" she asked Meredith.

"He said he had something to do," Meredith reassured her. "I'm sure he'll be here soon."

Elena nodded. Tension still hung over her, over all of them. Trinity was balanced between life and death now, they all knew it, and the only thing they could do was to wait.

* * *

Matt scrubbed fiercely at the blood on his face with a wet wipe he'd found in the glove compartment of his car. He met his own gaze in the rearview mirror, confused and desperate, and looked away in frustration.

If he went into the hospital with blood on his shirt and in his hair, they'd either arrest him or try to operate on him.

Maybe there was something in his trunk. Hunching his shoulders so that no one in the hospital parking lot would realize he was covered in blood, he unearthed a dirty gray hoodie and pulled it over his head.

The emergency room was lit so brightly lit that it hurt his eyes for a moment. He staggered, blinking his eyes rapidly to adjust, and looked around. Before he could make it to the nurse behind the desk, Jasmine's voice spoke behind him. "Matt? What's going on?"

He turned to see her standing there, crisp and competent in her white coat, the complete opposite of everything he felt right now. When she saw his face, her eyes widened and she pulled him to the side of the room. "What is it?" she asked urgently. "What's happened?"

Matt licked his lips nervously. On the ride over, all he'd been able to think was: *Get Jasmine. She can help Trinity. You need Jasmine.* And she could help; he knew she could. But he didn't know what to say now.

"Please," he managed, his voice cracking. "Please, we have to hurry."

Jasmine frowned and glanced toward the admitting desk, and Matt angled himself to block her view. "No," he said. "We can't do this here. There'll be too many questions. You have to come with me now."

"Take a breath and tell me what's going on," Jasmine said calmly. Then she got a good look at him, and her eyes widened. "You have blood on your face." She reached out to touch him, clearly worried. "Where are you hurt?"

"It's not mine." Matt took a deep breath, feeling as if he was flinging himself off a high cliff over dark water. If he did this, there was no going back. But he had to. Trinity's life was at stake. "Please, trust me. I'll explain on the way. Vampires are real. Magic is real. A friend is hurt, and we can't bring her here."

Jasmine's eyes flew toward the admitting desk again, and the security guard beside it. "*Please*," Matt said desperately. "I need your help."

He gazed pleadingly at Jasmine and reached for her hand, trying to throw all the love he felt for her into one look, trying to remind her of how she trusted him. It was a lot to ask. But even if she thought he was having a psychotic break, he didn't mind, as long as he could get her to come help Trinity. She needed a *doctor*.

Jasmine looked doubtfully between him and the security guard, then finally sighed, her eyes softening. "I'll tell my supervisor I have to leave for personal reasons, and I'll come," she said. "But afterward, Matt, if I ask you to come back to the hospital with me, you're coming."

Matt pulled her into a hug, clinging to her, breathing in the scent of her, the normality and sanity she meant to him. "I'll wait for you out front," he said. "Bring a medical kit if you can. And please hurry."

othing was killing these vampires.

Damon grabbed one by the neck and sank a stake into his heart. His opponent fell, but instead of dying like he should have, he simply pulled the stake out of his chest, scrambled back to his feet, and lunged toward Damon again. *What the—?* Before the strange vampire could get close enough, Katherine grabbed him from behind and snapped his neck.

The vampire fell like a stone, but by now Damon knew that was only temporary. Breaking their necks kept these vampires down for longer than anything else they'd tried, but it wasn't permanent. Damon knew from experience that they had about half an hour before that vampire would be up and fighting again.

He glared down at the circle of temporarily incapacitated vampires around him. "What the *hell*?" he growled, kicking at one of them. "Stakes don't kill them, breaking their necks doesn't kill them, it's impossible to pull their heads off or their hearts out, they can walk in the daylight, and apparently they're not affected by holy ground." He gestured around at the baroque-style Russian Orthodox church they were standing in. Some older vampires still refused to go on holy ground, and it had been worth trying. "*How* are we supposed to kill them?"

"We'll find something," Katherine said grimly. "Let's search the bodies while they're out." She looked tired, Damon thought, her beautiful lapis lazuli eyes sunken and a slight grayish pallor to her skin. She wasn't getting enough to eat, he knew, and she was still letting him feed from her.

Damon used the toe of his extremely expensive—but now, to his dismay, badly scuffed—boot to flip over the vampire closest to him, an East Asian man with short dark hair. "Nothing worthwhile here," he said, going through the fallen vampire's pockets. "A few coins."

"This one's pockets are empty," Katherine reported, bending over another at the other end of the room.

"This one looks like a peasant." Damon glared haughtily down at the next unconscious vampire, who was dressed in ripped jeans and a stained T-shirt. "Terrible taste in clothes." Starving and running for his life made him more irritable than usual.

"We were more discerning when we turned people in the old days." Katherine sniffed. "You and Stefan were the only ones I made for centuries."

"You made up for it these last few years, though, didn't you?" Damon asked absently. Was there something in the peasant's pocket? His fingers closed on a narrow rectangle of cardboard, and he pulled it out. A business card. There was no phone number or address or any information at all, really. Just a company name—Lifetime Solutions—and a stylized black-and-white figure eight. "An infinity symbol?" he asked aloud. "Katherine, this—"

As he looked up, there was a sudden flurry of movement, and Katherine made a high, choking sound, her eyes startled wide open. There was a wooden stake buried in her chest.

One of the vampires who should have still been unconscious had risen up behind her, utterly silent, and attacked Katherine from behind. Katherine stared at Damon for one long moment, her lips parted in surprise. And then she fell.

Horrified, Damon flew across the room quickly enough to catch her before she hit the floor. Cradling Katherine carefully in the crook of one arm, he snapped the other vampire's neck again before it could stake him, too. The strange vampire hit the floor with a thud as Damon turned his full attention to Katherine.

"No, darling, stay with me," he begged, the shock hitting him. He pulled the stake from her chest, but he could tell already that it was too late. Her beautiful blue eyes were glazing over as he watched. Time seemed to stretch out as Damon thought of the long roads they'd traveled together, him and Katherine. From his days as a human, when he'd loved her with all his heart, to now, when they had become companions, even friends. Sharp, spiteful, sometimes charming, never boring. His Katherine.

"Damon," she breathed, just a whisper of sound. His chest tight with sorrow, Damon watched as the life in Katherine's eyes faded, and she went heavy and still in his arms.

He held her close for a moment, then slowly lowered her to the ground, stroking her cheek in silent apology. His eyes felt hot. He'd loved Katherine, and then he'd hated her. He'd died and killed for her, and he'd watched her die once before. Lately, she'd been his friend. His mind kept coming back to that. He didn't have many friends. He never had. "I'm sorry, Katherine," he whispered to her.

He kneeled, gazing down at her body, which looked painfully small and still on the floor of the church. She'd always loomed so large to him, his maker, his first love. "They'll pay for this," he swore solemnly. "I'll find a way to kill them. I promise."

One of the vampires on the floor stirred, and Damon slammed the stake in his hand through its chest. It wouldn't kill the vampire, Damon knew that, but it would keep him down a few minutes longer. They were recovering faster than they had the first few times he and Katherine had fought them. Wasn't *that* a wonderful thing to realize, he thought bitterly, now that he was alone.

Alone. Damon thought briefly of his brother, and anger whipped through him. Damon had asked Stefan to come. If he had been there, they wouldn't have been quite so outnumbered, and maybe Katherine wouldn't have died.

It was time to go. Damon got to his feet and scooped Katherine up in his arms, cupping her head carefully with one hand to hold it against his shoulder, her hair soft under his fingers. She was as light as she'd been the first day he'd met her, when he had lifted her down from her father's carriage. She'd looked shyly at him through dark lashes, and his human heart had sped up, filled with emotions he'd barely understood. They'd been such children then.

He was going to take these strange, almost unkillable vampires down, no matter what. As Damon pushed his way through the front double doors, his footsteps echoing in the vast empty space of the church, he felt for the business card in his pocket. Lifetime Solutions. It was as good a place as any to start.

#TVD11FarewellKatherine

* * *

On the apartment's balcony, Stefan closed his eyes for a moment. It was almost morning, and he was tired. Solomon was dead now, and Elena was safe. He wondered how long it would take for that to really hit him, for the gaping pit of anxiety he'd been carrying inside to heal.

A cool dawn breeze brushed his cheek, and just for a moment, it felt almost like a hand. It carried a fresh scent with it, the smell of damask roses. Stefan frowned.

Back at the beginning, when he'd been alive, Katherine had smelled like that. She used to bathe in rose water. It had been a long time since he'd smelled that scent—it wasn't the kind of perfume modern women wore.

Good-bye, Stefan. He didn't know if he really heard the words, but suddenly they were there in his mind. Katherine's voice. In a flash he knew what had happened, and his chest tightened with sorrow. Katherine was dead. She'd been his enemy those last times he'd seen her, but once upon a time he'd loved her.

He pushed the thought away. *I'm just tired and morbid,* he told himself, but something in him felt that it was true. He needed to call Damon to make sure he was okay.

Entering the living room from the balcony, Stefan almost ran into Jasmine, who flinched backward. "Sorry, oh, I'm sorry," she said, breathlessly.

Stefan stepped deliberately away from her, his hands held up in what he hoped was a nonthreatening gesture.

"No, excuse me," he said. Earlier, Matt had made Stefan show Jasmine his fangs and his speed to convince her that he was a vampire, and she'd coped with it all surprisingly well. Matt followed Jasmine in from the bedroom and put a reassuring hand on her shoulder.

Elena, Jack, and Meredith, who had been talking quietly on the sofa, jumped to their feet at Jasmine's arrival.

"How is she?" Elena asked.

Jasmine smiled wearily. "Trinity's stable," she said. "I set her up with some saline to keep her from getting dehydrated, and the tranexamic acid helped with the bleeding. I'm going to leave some antibiotics with you that she should take twice a day for the next week and a half, but I think she'll be fine." Her eyes flittered hesitantly back to Stefan. "The—what you gave her, the blood, really helped her heal. I don't think she would be alive without it."

Jack clapped Stefan on the shoulder, and Elena threw her arms around Jasmine. "Thank you," she said. "Thank you so much." Matt grinned and hugged Jasmine, too, and then Meredith piled on, all four of them laughing now, loose with relief.

Stefan smiled, keeping his distance, but a great wave of gratitude washed over him. If Trinity lived, if she recovered, then they would have come through this amazingly unscathed.

After a little more talk, all of them promising to help with Trinity's care, make sure she stayed in bed and took all her medications, Matt and Jasmine headed for the door. "Jasmine's working the emergency room again tomorrow," Matt said. "She'd better catch all the sleep she can. Meredith, do you want a ride?"

Meredith nodded. "Just let me grab my stuff," she said. "It's in the bedroom." She put a finger to her lips. "I won't wake her, I promise. Hunters can be as quiet as cats."

Jasmine rested her head on Matt's shoulder as they waited. Jack headed for the kitchen. "I'm going to tell the others," he threw back over his shoulder.

Alone for a moment, Stefan took the opportunity to pull Elena aside, to tell her about the strange moment out on the balcony. "When I was outside—" he began.

But before he could continue, feet pounded down the hall and Meredith burst back into the living room, her olive skin unnaturally pale. "Trinity's gone!"

19

"**We**'ll find her. We will find her," Matt said, pushing his foot down on the accelerator. He wasn't sure whom he was trying to convince, Jasmine or himself, but even he could hear the uncertainty in his voice. How could anyone have gotten to Trinity? She'd only been unattended for a couple of minutes at most. There'd been no sign of violence in the room, just the covers pushed back, the saline drip making a wet patch on the empty bed.

"I can't understand how she could have walked away." Jasmine shivered. "She was so sick. She just kept staring at me with those yellow eyes while I gave her the injections. I doubt she even saw me."

"I don't think she left on her own," Matt said tightly. The sun was just coming over the horizon, dazzling him, and he squinted hard at the road ahead. Then the other part of what Jasmine had said registered, and his hands jerked on the wheel.

"Careful!" Jasmine yelped, and Matt swerved back into his own lane, his heart pounding.

"What do you mean, yellow eyes?" he asked. "Trinity has blue eyes; I'm sure of it."

Shaking her head, Jasmine wrapped her arms around herself. "This is all too weird," she muttered, and fell into silence for the rest of the ride home.

When they got to Jasmine's building, Matt parked and walked Jasmine to her door. She turned to him, her key in her hand, and his heart sank. There was something unfamiliar in her face: a look of fear and doubt. *I did this. I wanted to keep all this from her so she'd never have to look like that.*

"Trinity will be all right," he said, babbling, desperate to take that look away. "We'll find her tomorrow; everything will be fine. She can't have gone far. And, you know, she'll be all right because *you* saved her. I can't—I'm so grateful to you, I can't tell you how much—"

But Jasmine was shaking her head back and forth in denial, a strong *no no no.* "Matt—" she said.

"I love you," Matt said quickly, talking over her. "It's not always like this, I promise. And we can teach you to protect yourself." Matt reached out a hand, trying to reassure her, but her arms were crossed over her chest.

That was the wrong thing to say; he knew it as he said it. Jasmine's lips twisted into a wry smile. "That's supposed to make me feel better?"

Matt's vision blurred. "I love you," he said again, hearing the flat note of despair in his voice. He always lost everything. Everyone.

Jasmine's eyes were shining with tears. She uncrossed her arms and reached out to take Matt's hand. "I love you, too, Matt," she said, steadily. "But this is too dangerous, for both of us." She frowned. "Maybe I can finish my residency somewhere else. We could start fresh."

Matt stepped back. "I can't just *leave*," he said. "These are my friends. We have to find Trinity and figure out—" He broke off. Jasmine's face was miserable with longing, but her mouth was a firm line.

"I know," she said, her fingers tightening on his as if she couldn't bear to let him pull away. "You're so loyal. I love that about you."

"So . . . is this the end?" he asked her, dreading what she would say next. He felt like he was drying up inside, withering.

"I think it has to be," Jasmine whispered. Tears were running down her cheeks, and she let go of his hand again to swipe at them, sniffing.

Part of Matt wasn't surprised. All this time, he'd known that it would come down to this—his friends, or Jasmine.

He couldn't have both. Love didn't work out for him. He ducked his head down, stared at his grimy sneakers. "I don't want to lose you," he said softly, "but I can't change who I am."

There was a choked-off sob from Jasmine, and then her lips brushed lightly over his cheek. He didn't look up, just kept his eyes fixed on the tattered shoelaces on his right shoe, the rip in the side. Then she was gone, the door of her building slamming behind her.

Matt touched the spot where Jasmine had kissed him, holding onto this, the last kiss she would give him. The sun had risen over the horizon now, and everything seemed hard and cold and bright.

He turned and walked back to the car alone, the wind whipping against his cheeks where he could still feel Jasmine's kiss.

he motel room Trinity had been sharing with Darlene didn't seem to hold any immediate clues. It was small and sort of grimy: There was barely enough room for all of them to fit inside. Jack and Darlene were rifling through Trinity's possessions while Stefan and Elena searched the furniture for anything hidden. Zander and Shay were mostly hanging around the kitchenette, doubtlessly searching for scent clues, and Meredith herself was examining Trinity's weapon collection.

The others were mostly out patrolling the town and the woods, the Pack's sharp noses trying to root out any scent that might lead them to Trinity. Matt hadn't shown up yet. He was probably on his way from Jasmine's now.

This is what it's like to be a traveling hunter, Meredith thought, looking around. She and Stefan had traveled in search of Old Ones, of course, but only for a few days at a time. This room was different. Everything in it, from the hard-wearing, neutral-colored clothes to the neatly kept weapons, could be packed quickly and easily into one duffle bag. These were the possessions of a girl constantly on the road.

Meredith reached into the weapons bag and ran her thumb over the handle of Trinity's spare machete. The grip was worn with use.

"I don't think she's been back," Darlene said, rifling carefully through a bureau drawer. Her face was creased with concern. "All of her clothes are here."

"These papers just have to do with the hunt," Jack said from the desk. "Nothing I don't have. Would she have gone back to her family, do you think? Maybe if she was confused from the blood loss?"

Darlene shook her head, her eyes fixed on Trinity's meager possessions. "Her parents were killed in a vampire attack a couple of years back. There's no one else."

Stefan's hands paused for a moment in their careful examination of the space below Trinity's mattress, where he was feeling for anything hidden. It was the tiniest flinch, but Meredith saw it. She knew how much human deaths at the hands of other vampires bothered him, even now that he'd killed so many monsters, saved all of their lives so many times. Stefan, she thought, had never forgiven himself for what he was.

Elena laid a comforting hand on Stefan's shoulder and said idly to Jack, "I thought you'd all known one another all your lives."

"Not Jack," Darlene told her. "He recruited us for this hunt out of Atlanta about a year ago. We've been after Solomon ever since."

"We're all from hunter families, though," Jack said, "and that's a bond that crosses state lines." He grinned at Meredith, and something warm expanded in her chest at the acceptance in his eyes: She and Jack and Darlene, they were all hunters.

She stood and zipped Trinity's weapons bag back up. It didn't hold any clues. "If only Bonnie were here. She does a great tracing spell. I'll have Alaric call her, and she can talk him through it."

Stefan nodded. "That's probably our best option."

Darlene closed the bureau drawer. "Guess we should go," she said, but she hesitated, looking around the room one more time. Her face was tight with anxiety. "I just don't know where she could have gone," she said softly.

Zander cleared his throat. He and Shay were hovering in the kitchenette, and something in the way they were standing made the hairs suddenly stand up on the backs of Meredith's arms.

"Are we sure Solomon's dead?" Zander asked, sounding reluctant, rocking back on his heels.

Stefan and Meredith glanced at each other.

"We all saw him die," Meredith said, puzzled. "You saw, too. Stefan cut him in *half*."

"Wait, do you *smell* him?" Elena asked, horrified. One of her hands pulled back in front of her chest, as if to stave off a blow. "You said all the scents in here were old," she protested.

Shay shrugged. "In here, yeah."

Zander shifted from one foot to the other, looking uncomfortable and anxious. "The smells in here are old," he said, "but back at your apartment, Trinity didn't smell right. It's kind of hard to explain. Like, her scent and Solomon's scents were all wrapped up together. I didn't worry about it then, because we were all just focused on how hurt she was, but now . . ."

He rubbed the back of his neck with one hand, and Meredith suppressed a little flare of annoyance. Bonnie usually acted as a Zander translator for the rest of her friends. Meredith hadn't really noticed until Bonnie went away that the guy wasn't the best at communication.

"Of course Trinity smelled like Solomon," Meredith said, trying to sound patient. "He was touching her at the Plantation Museum. And when Stefan killed him, his blood went all over her."

"Not like that," Zander said, frowning. "His scent wasn't on top of hers; they were all mixed up together.

That's not how it works." He looked at Shay and she gave him a little shrug, as if to say, *this is your thing, not mine.* Turning to Stefan, he said, "Is there any way he could have infected Trinity with something? Like, with some aspect of himself? Can Old Ones do that?"

Say no. Meredith looked at Stefan for reassurance, but he frowned, unsure. "The Old Ones have so many Powers that other vampires don't," he said slowly. "I never heard of anything like that, but it could be true."

Jack shook his head decidedly. "I've been hunting Old Ones for a while—longer than you, Stefan, no offense. None of them could do that."

A flicker of movement outside the window caught Meredith's eye. "Matt's here," she said. She opened the door, and Matt came in, red-eyed and unshaven.

"Are you okay?" Meredith asked. They were all tired and worried, but Matt looked even worse than the rest of them, shockingly pale and grim under his stubble, his face almost paper white.

"Fine," Matt said, but he sounded distracted. He looked at Stefan. "Listen, Jasmine said Trinity's eyes were yellow when she was treating her. I don't . . . what do you think that means?"

Goose bumps crawled up Meredith's skin. "Possession?" she said, her voice sounding strangely high to her own ears. "With the eyes, and the scent? Even though Solomon's dead?"

Stefan frowned. "He was doing *something* to Trinity before we managed to kill him. And the way he went around to all of us in the room, like he was testing us. It could have been a spell, some kind of blood ritual."

Jack stood. The way he pulled his shoulders back, his weight evenly balanced between his feet, reminded Meredith of how he'd looked when they were sparring. But the enemy wasn't here to fight. "What are you trying to suggest?" he asked.

Elena swallowed. "He's saying that when Solomon was in danger, he might have . . . moved into Trinity's body."

"If that were true," Stefan said, thinking aloud, "if he's really possessing Trinity right now, then all we've done is make him angrier. Make him want revenge." Stefan's eyes were fixed on Elena, and Meredith knew whom he was most worried about.

Elena's own mouth, however, had dropped open the moment Stefan said *revenge*. She looked around the circle of faces, her eyes wide with terror. "Where's *Andrés*?"

* * *

On the porch of James's old house, Elena dug in her purse for her keys.

"I didn't know you guys kept this house," Spencer said cheerfully. "Sweet." Zander had sent the younger werewolf along with Elena, Stefan, and Meredith while the rest of the Pack searched the woods, but Spencer seemed pretty casual about it. He'd always been sort of a preppy frat-boy type, perpetually tan, collar popped. He wasn't Elena's favorite werewolf.

"James left it to Andrés in his will," she explained tightly, finally unearthing the keys. "It comes in handy for Guardian business." In this case, "Guardian business" mostly meant that Andrés had a place to stay when he visited Dalcrest, as did Aunt Judith and Elena's little sister, Margaret.

Elena thought fondly for a moment of James. He'd been her professor at Dalcrest and had helped her ease into her life as a Guardian. She owed him so much.

But she couldn't help remembering, too, that this house was also the place where James had died. As Elena turned the key she tried to convince herself that her feeling of dread was misguided. Andrés had probably just overslept after everything that had happened last night.

The door swung open with a bang, and a rush of icy air chilled them. Spencer's and Stefan's heads shot up, both of them instantly on alert. It was as if they heard—or, God, *smelled*—something none of the humans could.

"Stay here, Elena," Stefan said, but she shook her head and moved forward with the others.

They found Andrés in the bedroom.

He was lying sprawled out across the flowered comforter, blood flooding the bed from the wide gashes in his torso. His face, however, was curiously untouched. His dark eyes stared into the distance, their long black lashes framing only blankness, and his mouth hung slack. One hand dangled off the bed, fingers pointing down. A trail of blood still ran sluggishly over his wrist and hand, dripping slowly onto the floor.

Elena buckled when she saw him, almost falling, but Meredith grabbed her and held her up. *Oh God oh God.* He'd been ripped apart, just like Sammy.

All around them sounded the steady drip of water as the ice on the windows and mirrors began to melt.

"Solomon was here," Stefan said. "We were right; he's not dead." His voice sounded almost dry and matter-of-fact, but Elena could hear the devastation underneath. They had all thought they were safe.

Elena stepped forward slowly, a sob escaping her throat. Meredith tried to hold her back, but she shook off her friend's grip. When she reached Andrés, she stood still and looked at him, trying to look past the gore to see her friend one last time.

Tentatively, she reached out to touch his hand, ignoring the sticky, lukewarm blood that coated it. Andrés's hands had always been in motion, graceful and expressive, reaching out to embrace the world. She remembered the day they'd met, when he had taken her hand in his, warm and strong and reassuring. They sat under a tree together, and he told her the truth about being a Guardian, and she had been less afraid.

Behind her, the others were murmuring together. Spencer had pulled out his phone and was calling someone, probably Zander. They were all tense and eager to hunt, she knew, but Elena wasn't ready to join them.

Andrés's eyes were dull now. They'd always been so bright. He'd been in love, for the first time, and somehow that seemed worse than anything, that he'd died here, thousands of miles away from his love.

Elena brushed her hand lightly over her friend's face, closing his eyes. "Good-bye, Andrés," she said quietly. It seemed so important to be gentle with him now, even though he wasn't really here anymore. "I'm so sorry."

#TVD11SolomonLives

21

"Damon, there's something *wrong* with you. I know it. I can feel it through our bond."

Damon listened as Elena took a ragged breath, sounding tearful. "Are you okay?"

"Damon, please call me. I'm worried about you."

"Damon, I don't even know if you're getting these messages. If you are, call me. Please."

Clicking "delete" on the last of the many messages from Elena that had filled up his voice mail, Damon leaned back to rest against one of the small peaked roofs of the Musée d'Orsay. A stiff night breeze lifted his hair, and he huddled into the collar of his jacket. Normally the cold wouldn't bother him at all, but he hadn't fed since Katherine died, and he was starting to feel it.

This was a good spot to rest. He hadn't yet seen any of the vampires that were chasing him shape-shift or fly, so for whatever reason, they must not be able to. And from here Damon had a fine view over the rooftops of Paris, the river Seine at his back. There would be plenty of warning if anyone came after him. Finally, a moment to catch his breath and listen to his messages.

Elena liked Paris, he remembered; she had visited when she was a schoolgirl. Maybe she'd even been to the Musée. He remembered when this building had been a train station, modern in every detail at the beginning of the twentieth century: elevators, underground tracks, and above, a great sunlight-flooded space. It had seemed impossibly new to Damon at the time.

He shook his head, dismissing the memory. He'd been feeling melancholy and sentimental lately, ever since he'd said good-bye to poor Katherine's empty body, leaving it buried in a churchyard—the least he could do for her. He was angry, and tired of running, and most of all, he was *hungry*.

But not lonely. He was never lonely, Damon reminded himself. Vampires weren't meant to travel in packs. Still, it would be nice to hear Elena's voice again.

When he called, she picked up immediately. "Damon? Are you okay?" Her voice was thick with tears, and he stiffened automatically.

"What's wrong, princess?" he asked, peering over the side of the museum. Was that a vampire far below, moving purposefully toward him? He sent his Power questing, found nothing. Sometimes they seemed to turn up out of nowhere, and he wasn't good at sensing this new kind of vampire at all.

"Andrés is dead," Elena told him, her voice cracking. "We think . . . the Old One we thought Stefan and Andrés killed, he's not dead after all. And he murdered Andrés." She gave a desolate little sob that went straight to Damon's heart.

"Oh, Elena," Damon said softly. "I'm sorry. I know you cared for him." The Guardian had been a friend to Elena, and, for that, Damon found it in himself to feel sorry he was gone.

Wait a minute. The Old One had been strong enough to trick Stefan and murder a Guardian?

Damn Stefan, anyway. He had told Damon that everything was fine.

"Stefan couldn't kill the Old One?" he asked, his eyes fixed on the walkway below. There were definitely more figures gathering there.

"It wasn't Stefan's fault," Elena argued. Damon sighed. Elena would always defend Stefan.

"But that doesn't mean it's okay," he said. "Stefan thought he was in control, and he wasn't. He told me you'd be fine."

Damon got to his feet, keeping a careful eye on the little knot of people—or vampires?—far below. Straightening his jacket, he realized his hands were shaking slightly. It was so *typical* of Stefan. He wasn't as careful as he thought he was.

"Nothing's ever Stefan's fault, is it?" he went on, surprised at the bitterness in his own voice. "I asked him to come out here to help us, and he said *no*. And now Katherine's dead. He said he would protect you, you and all your little human friends out there wallowing in small-town America, and now they're dying."

Elena sucked in a short, horrified breath. "Katherine's dead?" she asked.

"Yes," Damon said. He could hear Elena starting to cry again. Belatedly, he tried to soften his tone. Katherine and Elena, he had forgotten they had their own tie. "We just . . . weren't enough to fight what's after us, not this time. I asked Stefan to help, but he wouldn't come. I'll kill them, though, I promise you that."

"I had no idea," Elena said bleakly. "I'm so sorry, Damon. I know how much she meant to you."

For a moment, Damon was surprised that Elena knew how he'd felt about Katherine, when he'd only just figured it out himself. But of course Elena knew; she could feel everything he felt. He pressed his fist against his chest, letting the ache of sorrow pass between them.

"She and Stefan were the only ones left," he said. "The only ones who knew who I used to be. Now there's only Stefan."

Elena sighed softly through the phone, thousands of miles away, and Damon felt her sympathy like a warm pulse in the bond between them.

The group down below was streaming into the museum. It was dark and silent inside; these were no tourists. Time to go. "Elena, I can't talk," he said, speaking quickly, slamming shut her link to his emotions. "I'll call again soon."

He clicked the phone off and tucked it into his pocket, ignoring her call of "*Damon*!" Closing his eyes, he searched for his Power and pulled it around him.

For a moment, he didn't think he would be strong enough. He was so tired and hungry. He'd raced across most of Europe in the past few weeks, trying to get away from these nearly unkillable vampires, but they just kept coming. He could hear footsteps on the grand staircase of the museum, far below. Maybe Paris was as good a place as any to die one more time.

No. Fiercely, he dug deep in himself for more Power. He was *Damon Salvatore*. He was an aristocrat, a gentleman, a vampire. No one was going to bring *him* to his knees.

In his rage, he found what he needed. Long before his pursuers reached the roof of the museum, Damon had stretched his wings and flown into the darkness.

* * *

Elena couldn't breathe. Andrés dead. Katherine dead. Trinity dead, or possessed—who knew how much of her was still in there?

Damon had asked Stefan to help him, and Stefan had said no. Why hadn't he told her?

She was gripping her phone so tightly that its edges hurt her hand. Carefully, she hit the off button and put it down. Then she went to find Stefan.

He was sharpening the machete, the long-bladed weapon propped carefully against his knee as he slid a file along it.

"I need some more blood from you for the weapons," he said without looking up. "If Solomon's still out there, we need to go after him."

"Damon just called," Elena told him. "Katherine's dead."

Stefan's hand jerked, slicing a long cut on his arm with the machete, and he gave a small cry of pain. But his leaf-green eyes were unsurprised. "I know," he said. "I've known since it happened."

Elena found a cloth for him in the kitchen. "Here," she said. "Put some pressure on it." But the cut was already healing. Stefan just wiped the blood away and went back to sharpening the machete, his face closed off again.

"I thought—I felt something; I knew she was gone. How did she die?" he asked, his eyes on the blade. Elena knelt beside him and pressed her face against his shoulder, and he stopped sharpening the machete for a moment to rest his hand heavily against her hair.

"Damon didn't have time to say. I think something is chasing him." Elena drew back and watched Stefan keep moving the file steadily along the blade. Then she said, hesitantly, "He told me he asked you to come and help them. Days ago."

Stefan nodded, still not meeting her eyes. "I couldn't," he explained. "We were hunting for Solomon. I had to keep you safe."

"Stefan! Look at me." Stefan's head was still bowed, his gaze averted. Elena grabbed the handle of the machete and pulled it away from him. Stefan hissed in shock, yanking his hands back before it cut him again. Elena tossed the machete onto the floor.

"I am not that vulnerable," she said hotly. "I'm a Guardian, and I have Power of my own." Powerful and amazing, Trinity had called her. Elena knew she needed to remember that, to remember that she didn't need to be protected.

Getting to his feet, Stefan stared at her, stricken. "Andrés was a Guardian," he said. "And look what happened."

"And we weren't able to prevent it," Elena said. She was tired of this, tired of Stefan treating her like she was more vulnerable than the rest of them. Yes, Andrés had died, and it was terrible and frightening. Any of them could die, not just Elena. "All I'm saying is that I can take care of myself sometimes. And when I can't, there are people around me who can help. Meredith. The other hunters. A whole Pack of werewolves. I'm not alone."

Stefan reached out and took Elena's hands, pressing them against his chest, above his heart. "I had to be here," he said. "I want to protect you."

"It's not just about me," Elena said. "When Damon called you for help, you should have gone. He's your brother, and he needed you."

Stefan's mouth twisted into a bitter parody of a smile, still clinging to her hands. "It's always Damon, isn't it?" he asked. "Even when he's thousands of miles away, he manages to come between us."

Elena stared at him, and then she pulled away. "This has nothing to do with Damon. This is about *us*. I'm not something to protect. I'm a protector. We need to work together, and we need to keep the big picture in mind. I'm not the only person in the world, Stefan."

"To me you are," Stefan said, and reached for her again. Elena shook her head, her eyes filling with tears. How had they gotten to this state?

The room blurred around her, and she wiped her eyes. "Maybe you should sleep out here tonight," she said, her heart aching. "I need some room to breathe."

#TVD11TroubleInParadise

ear Diary,
    Stefan said that, to him, I'm the only person in the world.

There was a time when I would have loved to hear that. But now, it just makes my blood run cold.

He's out on the balcony, staring into the night, watching for danger instead of curling up in here with his arms around me. Most of me wants to run out there and apologize. He'd lose that miserable look he has, and we'd hold each other, and everything would be back to normal. For the night.

But when we woke up, the problem wouldn't be gone.

Everyone Stefan has ever loved—including me, including Damon—has died, and left him.

It breaks my heart how much Stefan has suffered, how it's almost impossible for him to believe that terrible things aren't about to happen.

Of course it's scary that Solomon's still alive, and still hunting me. But I'm a Guardian, and I'm strong in my own way.

I ought to be protecting everyone. That's what I'm here for, after all.

I keep worrying about Damon. If he asked Stefan for help, he must have really needed it, and Stefan would have known that. What's changed, that Stefan thinks protecting me is the only thing that matters?

I love him. So much. And I've never regretted choosing to drink the Fountain of Eternal Youth and Life, so that I could be with Stefan, forever.

I've never wondered if I made the right choice. Not until now.

"Looks quiet," Jack said, parking his van in front of the storage place. Row upon row of heavy metal sliding doors lined the walls of the huge concrete building, each marking a separate unit. "Our extra weapon stash is in row J. If Solomon's possessing Trinity and can access her memories, he might come here." He gave a half shrug as he unfastened his seat belt. "Worth a shot."

In the middle row of the van, Stefan closed his eyes wearily, just for a moment. He'd been dragging all morning, feeling like he was moving at half speed.

He was so tired. Elena's words still echoed in his mind: *I'm not the only person in the world, Stefan.*

To him, she was.

From her seat beside Stefan, Elena gave him a tiny, fragile smile. Stefan's chest ached a little at the peace offering. He smiled back, then, sighing, reached for the door handle. Tired or not, they needed to keep hunting Solomon.

"Wait a sec," Alaric said. "There's something you guys need to see." Leaning forward from the back row of seats, he handed Stefan a piece of paper. Zander craned his neck to get a better look, but Meredith, sitting between them, didn't react. She must have already known.

It was a computer printout of a "Missing" poster from the 1980s. Elena gave a sharp, high gasp when she saw it, and Stefan turned the paper so Jack and Darlene could see from the front as well. The photo was washed-out but recognizable: a young, sharp-featured man with tawny, shoulder-length hair, giving the camera an easy smile.

"That's Solomon," Zander said, cocking his head to one side. "Definitely. But the poster says Gabriel Dalton. I don't understand."

"When Meredith told me that you guys thought Solomon had possessed Trinity before he died, it didn't quite make sense," Alaric told them. "Possession doesn't work like that. If Solomon had his own corporeal body, the shock of it being destroyed would have jolted him right back out of Trinity. I thought something else might be going on, so . . ." He spread his hands, his eyes on the smiling photo of Gabriel Dalton. "I did some research. I think Solomon body-swapped into Trinity's body from Gabriel Dalton's, pulled her spirit out, and put his own in. The body we saw wasn't his original form either."

"This is proof that Solomon's done it before," Meredith said. "The body Solomon was using was once someone else's."

"So who did we kill in Solomon's—or, Gabriel's, body?" Jack asked, looking grim. "This Gabriel Dalton? Trinity?"

Alaric spread his hands in a *who knows?* gesture. "I think Gabriel Dalton's been dead for a while. Solomon wouldn't leave any loose ends, and if someone believed they were Gabriel Dalton in another form, it would make things . . . messier for him."

Stefan felt ill. Abruptly, he reached again for the door handle and hurried out of the van. He felt the others startle behind him, then follow toward the hunters' storage locker. *There's nothing you can do about it now*, he told himself. There was a bitter taste in his mouth. He'd thought killing Solomon was a triumph, but instead he'd murdered an innocent ally. He didn't want to believe it, but it felt true.

Jack fell into step beside him.

"I killed Trinity," Stefan said, defeated. Everything had happened so fast; he'd been so focused on killing Solomon, on ending all this.

"There's no way you could have known," Jack said roughly. "And Trinity was a good hunter; she knew the risks." He twisted a ring on his finger with an angry, abrupt gesture. "The important thing is that we know what form Solomon's in now. We should act quickly before he has time to swap into a body we *don't* know." He glanced back at Elena cautiously, then slowed to let her catch up. "Can you do that thing Andrés did? Channeling life force?"

Elena stopped dead and stared at him, aghast. "You mean *kill* her?" she asked angrily. "No. I won't. There's no proof that Trinity isn't still in there. She could be possessed, helpless while her spirit is controlled by Solomon." The others came up beside them, their faces worried.

A muscle at the side of Jack's mouth twitched, and Stefan broke in. "What do you suggest we do, Elena?" he asked. "Alaric believes this is a case of body-swapping, and Solomon's too powerful for us not to go after him with everything we have. If we hesitate, we put everyone in danger."

Elena's eyes narrowed. "By everyone, you mean me," she said tartly. "But Trinity matters, too. We need to *capture* her, not kill her. We can't kill her unless we're completely sure she's gone, that there's no trace of her left in her body."

His jaw clenching, Stefan glared back at her. For a moment, he felt like the world had narrowed to just the two of them. "You're not the only one threatened here," he said, his voice tense. "Think of Andrés. We can't risk everyone to save one person who is probably already dead."

"Yes, we can," Elena insisted. "We don't sacrifice innocent people to keep ourselves safe. That's not us, Stefan."

They stared at each other, Elena flushed and breathing hard.

"If there's a chance Trinity's still in there . . ." Darlene said slowly.

"She was a good hunter," Jack said again. "Trinity would give anything if it meant we killed Solomon."

There was a slight shifting in the room, as the group began to realize that there were two distinct sides, and they would all have to pick one. Jack agreed with him, Stefan knew: The risks of trying to capture Solomon without killing him were too high.

He'd fought with Elena before, over personal things, over Damon, but never over what the right course of action was. Looking at her outraged face, Stefan knew that if he ignored her, if he succeeded in killing Trinity, Elena might never forgive him. He could side with Elena, or he could keep her safe.

Either way, he might lose her forever.

eredith's eyes watered, blurring the harsh white lights, and she tried to turn her face away. But she was stuck fast.

This was worse than being held by Solomon's Power. She could feel the multitude of tiny wires pressing against her skin, holding her in their trap. Heart pounding, she strained against them, trying desperately to move. But after a moment she gave up, letting her muscles go slack. It was only a dream, and soon she would wake up.

It just felt so *real*. The table—she was almost sure now that it was an operating table, and that thought started a cold dread in the pit of her stomach—was hard beneath her. Peering through the corners of her watering eyes, she could make out the blurry shape of something cylindrical and silver by her bedside. An oxygen canister, maybe? Was this a hospital?

The thought made her forget to be calm. She struggled harder, trying to wake herself up. Meredith had always hated hospitals.

As she pushed desperately against her restraints, a shrill beeping sped up, faster and faster. A heart rate monitor.

There was a shadow moving in the corner. Meredith stopped thrashing about and strained to see, the heart monitor slowing a little. There was no doubt about it this time. It was a person—shadowy, but getting closer.

With a sudden step, the figure moved to stand above her, anonymous in a surgical mask and white lab coat. Meredith blinked, trying to focus, but the person's face was still blurry. Something sharp and metallic flashed in the stranger's hand.

A scalpel, Meredith realized, heavy with dread, and tried to scrabble backward, to press herself into the hard table below her. She couldn't move. Her breath was coming in anxious, harsh pants. "No," she cried out, suddenly able to speak, hating the pleading, pathetic sound of her own voice.

The blade flashed silver along her stomach as Meredith watched, its motion followed by a thin, spreading line of red.

Something terrible was happening to her. Panic scratched at the inside of Meredith's head, a frantic babble. Something terrible was happening *now*.

#TVD11Nightmares

* * *

Meredith's eyes shot open. Dark room, soft bed, Alaric's steady breathing beside her. She felt at her stomach, reassuringly whole and unbloodied. She'd *known* it was a dream. But her heart was pounding hard, and her mouth was dry. Dream or not, she'd brought the fear with her: *Something terrible is going to happen.*

She got out of bed and padded into the kitchen, leaving the overhead light off. When she opened the refrigerator to pull out the water pitcher, she winced, blinking at the brightness. Her eyes were still sensitive from the harsh white lights. *No*, she reminded herself. *They're not. That was just a dream.*

Her throat was as dry and sore as if she'd really been screaming, though. Meredith gulped down the water and poured herself a second glass. It felt good going down, icily cold, but when she finished she was still parched.

There was something off about her, she thought. She felt jittery and overly sensitive, as if a touch might be too much to bear.

Swallowing against the ache in her throat, she squared her shoulders. *Be strong.* She was probably feeling weak because she'd been slacking off on her exercise schedule. Patrolling with Jack and his hunters was no substitute for a real workout.

A run clear would clear her head, Meredith decided.

A few minutes later, she left the house wearing a ratty old T-shirt and shorts, her hair pulled back into a ponytail. Starting with a slow, deliberate jog, she gradually sped up, her feet slapping a steady rhythm against the sidewalk. The sky was beginning to lighten with the promise of dawn, but she had a stake strapped to her waist, hidden by her shirt, just in case.

By the time she reached the Dalcrest campus, she was almost at a sprint. The faster she went, the more centered Meredith felt, resettling comfortably in her own body again as her muscles strained.

The sun was just creeping over the horizon, and the campus was almost deserted. Meredith ran right past the only two people in sight, a couple making out, hot and heavy, pushed up against the side of the library.

A few strides farther on, she stopped, the scene she'd just passed replaying in her mind's eye. The way the girl had her face pressed into the man's throat, her arms holding him in place. The slump of the guy's shoulders.

Meredith swore and turned back, running as fast as she could, her hands fumbling to pull the stake from under her shirt.

It wasn't until the girl looked up, blood dripping down her chin, the ends of her hair sticky and matted, that Meredith realized it was Trinity.

"Hey there," she said, baring her teeth at Meredith. "I was hoping I'd run into *all* you hunters."

With a twist of horror, Meredith realized the guy Trinity held propped up was Roy, one of the hunter brothers. He flopped forward against her, his eyes closed and his head hanging limply. Meredith couldn't tell if he was breathing.

Her hands closed tighter over her stake, her heart pounding. If she could get close enough . . . A stake wouldn't kill an Old One, if that was even what Trinity was now, but it might slow her down.

"Are you in there, Trinity?" she asked, watching the girl carefully. If only she'd glance away for a moment. If Meredith could somehow distract her, maybe she could get close enough.

Trinity's smile grew, but she said nothing, just stuck out the tip of her pink tongue to lick the blood off her lips. With an internal shudder, Meredith realized Trinity's eyes were yellow now, like an animal's. Like Gabriel Dalton's when he had Solomon inside him.

Taking a step closer, the stake firm in her grip, Meredith asked, "Do you know who you are?" She cocked her head toward Roy, limp and still, his head lolling against Trinity's collarbone. "Do you know who *he* is?"

Trinity laughed, a harsh, sudden noise completely unlike her usual soft chuckle. "All you hunters are tied so tightly to one another, aren't you? I wonder if you know as much as you think you do."

She glanced at Roy for a moment. "This one? He's a fighter, but he couldn't strike at someone he knew." Meredith was only half listening. With Trinity's attention distracted for that split second, she saw her chance.

Lunging forward, she stabbed the stake at Trinity's heart.

And was frozen in place.

If Meredith harbored any doubts that Solomon had invaded Trinity's body, they fell away now. It was like the Plantation Museum, like her nightmares. Her muscles, which just a minute ago had been strong, running, were completely immobile.

"I'd kill you now, but it's more fun to play," Trinity— *Solomon*—said. "I'll see you around, hunter." She stepped away from the library without even glancing back at Roy, and he fell heavily to the ground, landing on the concrete with a sinister thud.

Without looking back, without hurrying at all, Trinity sauntered off, her boots clicking on the pavement. Meredith was powerless to do anything except watch her go.

When Trinity had turned the corner and was completely out of sight, the hold she had on Meredith broke.

Immediately Meredith raced after her, her heart pounding as she rounded the corner of the library and ran between the dorms behind it. But Trinity was gone. The campus spread out in front of her in the early morning light, peaceful and silent and completely empty.

Meredith went back to Roy. He was still lying where Trinity had dropped him, his tall, broad body looking small and broken.

Meredith turned him over gently and checked his pulse. Roy flopped over unresistingly, a dead weight, his throat torn and bloody. How had Solomon's invasion of her body turned Trinity into a vampire? Meredith didn't understand it, but the evidence was right here before her. Trinity was a vampire—and like all the Old Ones, one who had nothing to fear from daylight.

Poor Roy, Meredith thought. Had he been happy to find Trinity, before she turned on him? She placed her hands on his chest and began CPR, pushing in a steady rhythm, lowering her mouth to his to force oxygen into his lungs. Even though she was pretty sure it was pointless, she had to try.

When Stefan and Elena had argued earlier over Trinity's fate, Meredith hadn't known what to think. But now she knew Stefan was right.

Trinity hadn't known who Roy was, hadn't really remembered Meredith. They'd both just been hunters to her, targets Solomon had been aware of all along. The girl who had been their friend, who had hunted beside them, was gone.

24

"No matter what happens, we have to try to hang on to normal," Elena said.

Matt nodded. Personally, this was the last thing he wanted to be doing. But it was typical Elena: When things were at their worst, she whistled in the dark. He just wished Elena's way of whistling in the dark didn't include making Matt try on shirts.

"That one looks nice," she went on, giving him a friendly once-over. "I know Jasmine likes green."

Matt stiffened. He hadn't told anyone about what had happened with Jasmine yet. There was too much going on for him to feel like he could bring up his personal life, and he wasn't sure he was ready to talk about it. "We broke up," he said, his voice sounding just as rough and miserable as he felt.

"Oh, no," Elena breathed. "What happened?" Then her face darkened as she answered the question for him. "It's because she finally found out the truth about everything, isn't it?"

"Yeah," Matt said quietly. "She didn't want all that to be part of her life."

"I don't blame her." Elena grimaced. She bent her head and flicked distractedly through some more shirts. "It's terrifying. Remember how you felt when you found out that all of this—vampires and hunters and scary monsters in the dark—is real?" She looked up at Matt questioningly. "If you could do it all again, go back to the way things were before, would you?"

Matt flinched. *We could start fresh*, he heard Jasmine saying again, remembering how wide and pleading her beautiful eyes had been, and how they'd darkened in disappointment.

"I could never leave you guys in danger," he told Elena, and it was true.

Elena looked up at that. "I know you couldn't," she said, her mouth curling into a sad smile. "But I worry about you sometimes." She pulled two more shirts off the rack and shoved them into his hands. "Try on the blue one first and let me see."

In the dressing room, Matt carefully buttoned the blue shirt and smoothed it down. *Elena doesn't need to worry about me*, he thought. But how could he ever turn his back on his friends? It went against everything he believed in.

"Gorgeous!" Elena said when he came out in the new shirt. Her voice was cheerful, but her smile looked pasted on, too wide and toothy.

"How about you and Stefan?" Matt asked cautiously. "Today, the two of you seemed . . ." *Angry.* ". . . at odds."

Elena's smile fell. "He and Jack are out there, trying to track down Trinity," she said, her voice flat. "They asked if I could trace her aura, but I refused. Not unless they're going to try to save her before they kill Solomon." She let out a long, frustrated breath. "Stefan just won't listen. He thinks he's protecting me, but I'm not helpless."

"I know," Matt said gently. "Even before you were a Guardian, you were pretty tough." Elena rewarded him with a more genuine smile, and he went to change shirts again.

When he came out, she had a lock of her silky blond hair twisted around her finger, her face thoughtful. Pushing at the rack of shirts, she said, "Can't Stefan see there's more to the world than me?"

Matt couldn't help the bubble of laughter that rose up in his throat at that. "Sorry," he said, in response to Elena's frown, "but when we were in high school, that's the *last* thing you would have said."

Elena had the grace to chuckle a little at that. "I wasn't that bad," she replied defensively.

"Well, *I* always liked you." Matt shrugged. He had more than liked her—beautiful, selfish, determined Elena. He still liked her now, but somewhere along the way, he had finally given up on loving her.

"I've changed," Elena said. "We all have. We grew up. I'm *proud* of who I am now." She frowned, sticking her chin out stubbornly. "And I *cannot* let Jack and Stefan kill Trinity without even trying to save her."

"I know, and I'll help if I can." Matt hesitated, not sure whether to say the rest of what he was thinking, and Elena cocked an inquiring eyebrow. "Just . . ." He didn't quite know which words to use. "Just don't give up on Stefan, okay? You love each other, and that's . . . hard to lose. I don't like seeing you fight." He thought again of Jasmine's eyes when she'd said good-bye, and his chest felt hot and tight.

Something of this must have come through in his words, because Elena looked at him knowingly, terribly sad, her lips pressed together and a deep line between her eyebrows.

To make her smile again, he held up the blue shirt. "And I'm buying the shirt."

He didn't really need a new shirt, but it was worth it to see her face lighten. As he followed Elena to the check-out line, though, he couldn't help the nagging worry that always lived at the back of his mind now, that had lived there for years.

The worst is still to come.

* * *

When Elena got back home, Stefan was digging through the hall closet. "I'm looking for my axe," he explained, a bit awkwardly, not looking at her. "Have you seen it?"

Elena shook her head, and he shoved a bunch of coats aside. "Here we are," he said, pulling it out and turning away. "I need to go. I'm late meeting Jack."

"Stefan—" Elena reached out to stop him.

He turned back toward her, seeming reluctant. There was so much pain in his face, lines of strain around that perfect sensual mouth and hurt darkening his eyes, making Elena's heart ache. All the way home, she had been thinking of what Matt said: *You love each other, and that's hard to lose.*

"Stefan," she said, helplessly. "I don't want to hurt you. I *never*, ever want to hurt you. I love you so much."

Stefan's face softened and he stepped toward her. "I love you, too, Elena. Everything I do is for you."

"I know that," Elena said, her voice calm and even. She smiled at him and held out her hand, feeling like she was coaxing some small animal out of its hiding place. He took it, hesitantly, and she squeezed, her palm warm against his. "I'm sorry we argued. But I'm worried about you. I'm afraid wanting to protect me has kept you from seeing how someone as innocent as Trinity—the *real* Trinity—needs us to give her a chance."

Stefan opened his mouth to object, and Elena pushed on quickly. "I worry that your morals are getting out of whack, Stefan, because you're so worried about me that you're not stopping to think. It's what I've always admired most about you, your sense of right and wrong," she finished softly, and rose up to brush her mouth against his.

But Stefan pulled away. "I love you, too, Elena," he said. He was frowning, his face hard with determination. "But we have to stop Solomon before he kills again. If that means losing Trinity, that's the price we have to pay. If we had any proof, any sign at all that Trinity was still in there, I'd be with you on this. But all I see in there is Solomon."

"We need to give her a chance," Elena said, her voice rising. "It's not fair. I know I don't have any proof, but we aren't *sure*. If there's even a shred of a chance that Trinity's trapped in there, we have to do everything we can to save her." She'd tried to talk to Stefan with a cooler head, but here they were, right back where they'd started.

Stefan turned away and headed for the door, his axe swinging easily from his hand. "I'm sorry, Elena, but I can't promise you that," he said coldly over his shoulder. "I have to do what's right, what's best for everyone. Even if you can't see it." He closed the apartment door quietly behind him.

Elena stared after him, her heart aching. He shouldn't have to shut himself off from her like that. She was losing Stefan—and he was losing himself.

25

"**R**eady?" Bonnie asked, reaching for Marilise and Rick. They each joined their free hands with Poppy's, forming a circle of four.

Poppy blinked rapidly, clearly nervous, and Bonnie grinned at her reassuringly. They all could feel Alysia watching them from the other side of the roof and, behind her, the other groups with their mentors.

Bonnie swallowed and steeled herself, shutting out everything except her three friends and the cool stone of her falcon resting at the hollow of her throat. She used it to center herself, breathing deeply, and closed her eyes.

Her consciousness flickered along their joined hands, going around the circle, pulling on Marilise's solidity, Poppy's energy, Rick's calm. To each of them, she said, silently, *Can I? Can I? Let me in*, and felt each reply a wordless *yes*. Their hands warmed in hers, and she waited.

And then Bonnie felt a little thrill along her spine as something slid into place between them, all their edges neatly fitting together. With a jolt, they were connected. Power began to pour into Bonnie from all three, filling her, making her gasp. She was a balloon, swelling with the others' Power, stretched so thin it was almost too much for her to contain.

Bonnie opened her eyes—or rather, opened several pairs of eyes, each in a different place. She saw the far-away stars glowing faintly above the city from four different angles. She could see her own profile through their eyes, her head tilted backward, her cheeks round and soft. Bonnie felt like a live wire, thrumming with the energy of four people, burning and fizzing with it.

She took all this Power, her own and her three partners', and gave it a direction. It roared fiercely through her and up toward that clouded, dim-starred city sky. Flooding through her body and expanding farther and farther out, the Power cleared away the clouds, brightening the stars.

Bonnie gasped for breath and kept pushing. Power pulsed steadily through her as she concentrated on summer back home, picnics down at Warm Springs when she was in high school, the sun hot on her back and the smell of fresh-cut grass underfoot. Mixed up with this were Poppy's memories of her days at summer camp, pounding along on horseback on a wooded trail; Rick's of a childhood creek, cold water splashing around his calves, sharp river pebbles underfoot and sticky humid heat wrapping around him like a blanket; and Marilise digging in her garden, fragrant plants and crumbling dirt under her hands.

All those summers combined into one. Bonnie felt it take shape—hot and long and glorious, a perfect summer— and then she *pushed* it into the night.

Slowly, a bright white light began to grow and grow on the rooftop, Bonnie at its center. A few querulous chirps sounded and then a growing cacophony of birdsong, as birds awoke and decided that they had somehow missed the dawn. Everywhere else, it was night, but here on the rooftop, surrounded by their joined Power, it was day.

Bonnie held the sun in place for a few minutes, locked into a circuit of their Power, which ran through her into the sky and back to them again. She *was* the circuit. She felt stronger and more flush with Power every moment. She could keep the false day going all night, she realized, until the real sun came up.

But then she pulled back, breaking the circuit. This was just a demonstration of what they'd learned; she didn't need to hold it all night. It was enough to know that she could. Power drained out of her, leaving her alone in her own head. She blinked as her vision reduced to one point of view, one set of eyes. The light faded slowly, and night fell again.

Bonnie let go of her friends' hands and snapped the connection between them, releasing their Power. Breathing hard, they smiled at one another.

There was a burst of applause and some murmurs of appreciation from the group behind them as they surged closer. Bonnie had almost forgotten about their audience. "Very nice, very nice indeed," an older, bearded man kept saying, nodding and patting them on the backs.

Alysia pulled Bonnie to the corner of the roof, grinning. "That was terrific!" she exclaimed. "I liked what you chose, the way you all pulled energy from a personal memory. It's much stronger that way. You're really good at this."

"Thanks," Bonnie said. "It felt . . . it was great, I felt like I *was* all three of them, sort of. And myself, too." She was alone in her head now, but she could still feel the echoes of them: Poppy's spirit, Rick's intentness, Marilise's warmth.

Alysia raised her hand and pushed one of Bonnie's wild curls out of her face. "I know you've been waiting to go home, and I think, now, you're ready," she said. "You've learned so much. Maybe it's time to use your Powers where they're really needed."

Happiness rose up inside Bonnie, making her feel almost weightless for a second. *Home!* Now she could really help with the trouble in Dalcrest, more than she ever had before. Now she could go back where she belonged. She'd get to be with the friends she loved as much as sisters, and with Zander, wonderful, clear-eyed, warmhearted Zander. She'd missed him with a constant low ache the whole time she'd been in Chicago.

Impulsively, she reached out and wrapped her arms around Alysia, pulled her into a tight hug. "Thank you," she said, smiling so hard her cheeks hurt, "Thank you so much."

* * *

If she concentrated all of her Guardian Powers, Elena could just see the faintest wisps of darkness, like tendrils of smoke hanging in midair. Eyes narrowed, she followed the traces of the dark aura, moving carefully from one to the next as she trekked through the woods. Matt and Darlene were following her, the undergrowth crunching beneath their feet, but she couldn't risk looking back at them. If she took her attention off the trail of evil stretching out before her, it just might disappear.

"Are you sure she knows what she's doing?" she heard Darlene whisper loudly to Matt.

"Yes," Matt answered, defensive. "Remember what Andrés did? Elena's special."

To be completely honest, Elena *wasn't* entirely sure she knew what she was doing. Stefan, Jack, Alex, and Meredith—four experienced hunters, one of them a vampire—had headed out to hunt Trinity today, weapons in hand, earpieces on, aiming for a kill. Zander had his werewolves patrolling the town and the campus, keeping people safe. Alaric was at the university, researching more folklore about body-swapping and possession.

And then there was the renegade force: Elena, Matt, and Darlene, hoping to somehow bring Trinity in alive. They wanted to hold her safe until they could figure out how to reverse what had happened and put Trinity back in control of her own body.

Darlene had appeared on Elena's doorstep that morning and grabbed her by the arm, her fingers as strong and tight as if they were made of iron. *Hunter's grip*, Elena had thought, trying to wriggle free. Meredith held tight like this.

"Jack told us you want to get Solomon out of Trinity," Darlene had said, fixing Elena with fierce dark eyes, something desperate in her tone. "I want to try, if you will. Trinity's like a little sister to me."

Of course Elena wanted to try. She remembered Trinity's laughing challenge to her on the roof at the apple orchard and felt a pang of sorrow—that sweet-natured girl was lost, and no one was going to help her. If there was even the slightest chance Trinity was still there, they had to try. *No matter what Stefan thinks, I need to do what's right*, she thought, trying to make herself strong and inflexible.

She wasn't used to being on the opposite side of an argument from Stefan.

So now here they were, just Elena, Darlene, and Matt, the three musketeers, hoping that somehow they could save Trinity. Following this trace of *wrongness*, these tiny shreds of darkness hanging in the air, Elena led them forward. The trail was thin and faint, but it was there.

The darkness led them through the woods away from campus, mostly downhill. Their feet squished unpleasantly in the mud.

At last they came to the edge of a lake. Little ripples wet the toes of Elena's boots as she followed the dark aura right to the shore. When she strained her eyes, she could see its trail leading out over the water, toward the vast middle of the lake.

"It goes straight over the water," she told the others.

"We're not going out there," Matt objected. "We'll walk around, pick it up on the other side."

Elena shook her head, her eyes on the faint traces of darkness. "If we leave the trail, I probably won't be able to find it again. It's too faint."

"Elena . . ." Matt said.

"I *can't*." She stared at him desperately. "We'll lose it."

Matt sighed. "I'll find a boat," he said, gesturing off to the right. "There's a boathouse over there."

Elena nodded, never taking her eyes from the dark trail, barely daring to blink. Behind her, she heard Darlene shift from foot to foot and sigh.

"I knew Trinity's family," the older hunter said. "Before her parents died, they were almost like my parents, too. They fed me, offered me a place to stay, gave me advice I usually didn't follow. Trinity . . . she's the only one left. I can't just let go of her."

"We'll do our best," Elena said, her eyes still fixed over the water. "I promise. I want to save her as much as you do." She was trying not to show it, but she was used to having Stefan, Meredith, and Bonnie on her side. With Bonnie gone and the others united against her, Elena felt so alone.

She gritted her teeth. She was doing the right thing, and that had to count for something.

There was a plashing of oars as Matt rowed up to them in a dented old rowboat. He jumped out and waded to shore, pulling the boat up behind him. "Here we go," he said. "There wasn't much selection. The crew team locks their boats up."

Elena sat in the front of the boat and pointed the way, while Darlene and Matt each took an oar.

As they traveled, the evil aura got darker and thicker. Elena was sure now that it was Solomon's. It felt ancient and cruel, like a bitter memory, something that had survived long millennia steeped in violence and hate. There was a strange yellowish-green mixed up in the smoky darkness, and Elena remembered what Jasmine and Meredith had said about Trinity's eyes.

As they neared the middle of the lake, the boat suddenly lurched. Elena yelped, grabbing hold of its side to keep her balance.

"What was that?" Darlene asked sharply.

"The wind must be picking up," Matt said, but there was a note of uncertainty in his voice.

The waves were getting bigger, tossing the boat angrily in the water. Elena gripped the sides so hard her fingers ached.

"There's no wind," Darlene said suddenly, and Elena realized she was right. The sky was black and ominous, but the air was still. The waves moved more violently, the front of the boat going up in the air and then smacking down onto the water with a sickening lurch.

Right in front of Elena, the aura she'd been following disappeared, dissolving into nothingness.

"It's a trick," she gasped, just as the boat smacked into the water hard, dumping them out.

Elena was pulled down, down, down under the water, her hair streaming out behind her like a mermaid's. *No,* she thought, *no, please, no.* She'd drowned once before, in the dark waters of the creek under Wickery Bridge. She'd *died.*

She kicked and thrashed, trying to swim up toward the surface, but it was as if some invisible force was pushing on her, sending her straight down. Her feet hit the muddy bottom and waterweed, soft as feathers, wrapped itself around her legs.

Holding her breath, she bent her legs and pushed off hard against the lake bottom, focusing on the dim light above. She could see shadows in the water above her— Matt and Darlene, and the vague outline of the boat.

She was so cold. Colder than made sense for a summer day, even in deep water.

The water had been cold the other time—the night she went off the bridge. Ice in her hair, the heavy painful push of water filling her lungs, the blackness that had sucked her in. The last thing she had seen was the hood of Matt's car swallowed by dark water.

I'm not going to make it. Elena pushed the thought away and kept swimming upward. Ice crystals were forming around her, she realized, sharp and crystalline.

She was about to break through when her hands hit something hard and flat and cold above her. She gasped in surprise, accidentally letting the water in, and red-and-black sparks burst in her vision. With the last of her strength, Elena pounded her fists against the barrier, felt for an opening. But it was no use.

The pond had frozen over above her. *Solomon.*

She tried to keep hitting at the ice, but she was floating down, down, toward the darkness below. *A human death*, she thought, and then, *Oh, Stefan, I'm so sorry to leave you this way.*

Some last spark in her flared in rebellion. She *wasn't* going to die like this, not again. She was a Guardian. Elena reached deep, deep inside herself and pulled hard at the last of her Power.

Something arced out of her, a pure white light, and with a sudden shock, the ice above her head cracked violently open. And somehow, with one last feeble kick, she managed to break the surface of the water.

She opened her eyes but for a moment, she still couldn't see. She was coughing, taking great rasping, greedy breaths, struggling not to slip back under. And then something grabbed her by the *hair*, was now holding her by the arms, and she started fighting it, turning and twisting blindly in the water.

"Elena! Elena!" There was a sharp pain across her face, and Elena stopped struggling, shocked. "Elena!" It was Matt, gripping onto one of her arms, his other hand raised to slap her again. Darlene, her wet hair matted, was clutching her other arm. The boat bobbed across the water next to them.

Tears streaming from her eyes, Elena clung to Matt, his body warm and solid next to her freezing one. She choked and gagged some more, spitting icy water. "It was a trick," she managed to say after a minute, sobbing.

"I know. I can't . . . I don't know what just happened, but I'm so glad you're okay." Matt gulped and took a deep breath, his arms tight around Elena. "We have to get back to shore."

Matt boosted Elena up, steadying the boat with one hand. With a lot of effort, she managed to wiggle back over the side, scraping her stomach uncomfortably, and land in a graceless heap on the bottom of the boat.

They rowed back toward shore. The waves were gone and the surface of the lake was still. The ice had already almost melted in the summer sun, but here and there bits of it bobbed on the lake surface, so beautiful that Elena could barely believe it had just tried to kill her.

Matt frowned. "Maybe Stefan is right. Maybe it's too dangerous to try to save Trinity."

"No," Elena said. Her head was pounding, her eyes burned, and her chest felt raw and painful, but she wasn't going to listen to an argument about this again. "We're not going to kill her. Not unless we know for sure that she's already gone."

* * *

"No sign here," Jack said, tapping his earpiece. "But Solomon doesn't usually leave evidence of kills. Stay north and keep your eyes open. We're heading southwest."

Meredith heard the murmur of Stefan and Alex's reply, and then they ended the transmission. Jack jerked his chin and she followed him southwest through the woods, scanning carefully all around them.

She caught sight of a mark in the mud underfoot and lifted a hand to get Jack's attention. "Footprints," she said, keeping her voice low just in case. The indentations were indistinct, but they looked about Trinity's size. Not many people would be walking this far back in the woods.

Jack kneeled down to examine them, his blue-jeaned knees sinking into the soft soil. "Not her." He gestured at the heel. "These are too big. Trinity has smaller feet than this."

"Oh," said Meredith, disappointed. They'd been searching the woods for a while, and so far, they hadn't found anything. No bodies, no sign of anything unnatural. "Sorry," she added, feeling useless.

"Solomon's always been incredibly talented at staying invisible," Jack said, as if he were reading her mind. "Andrés being able to find Solomon was the first break we'd had in a long time." He straightened up and shot Meredith a crooked smile. "Any chance we'll be able to talk Elena into trying again? I didn't know how handy a Guardian could be."

Meredith shook her head. "Elena won't help hunt as long as she thinks she might be able to save Trinity."

"Yeah, I see that." Jack's shoulders drooped and, for a minute, he looked very tired. "Trinity was a terrific hunter. But we have to accept that she's gone and what we're hunting is the vampire that killed her."

"I know," said Meredith. Her stave felt heavier than usual. There wasn't a lot of pleasure in this hunt, knowing that, at best, it would end in fighting something that had the shape of a friend.

They walked on in silence for a while. A couple of times, Jack stopped to check footprints on the forest floor, but both times shook his head and went on. Not Trinity's. Meredith kept her eyes peeled for any anomalies.

Then she spotted a familiar clump of plants: soft purple blossoms, branching green stems, and small-toothed leaves. "Look, vervain," she said, pleased, and unzipped the pack she carried on her back. The opportunity to restock their vervain supply wasn't something she would pass up. She began to pick the herb's shoots one by one, careful not to crush their blossoms.

"I haven't used vervain much," Jack said, coming closer to look. "But I should probably start putting it in tea or something, like you do. Does it hurt Stefan, though? To be around it?"

"Not really. Of course, he could never drink from any of us, but I don't think it would ever come to that." She paused. "It's important for the rest of us to keep our minds clear. We need all the defenses we can get."

Jack crouched down to examine the spindly plants more closely. "I never would have considered hunting with a vampire before now," he ventured. "Doesn't it bother you? What he is?"

Meredith straightened up. She'd picked all the plants but left the roots, just the way Bonnie had taught her. They'd grow again and she could come back to this patch for more. "Stefan's more than proven himself to me," she said flatly. "And he's not a killer. He doesn't feed on humans."

"I know that," Jack said. "He told me. Doesn't that make him weaker, though?" His dark eyes were intent.

"I guess, but he's pretty strong anyway. He's old, and vampires get stronger with age," Meredith said, suddenly determined to defend Stefan. She took a few steps farther into the woods, continuing their trek, then stopped and turned back to Jack, feeling a fierce, protective rush of heat inside her. "I *trust* Stefan. I might be a hunter, but I'm always going to be on his side."

Jack nodded and started walking again, shoulder to shoulder with her.

They walked in silence for a while after that. The day was getting hot, the sky a deep blue dome high above them. Meredith felt easier now, glad that she and Jack understood each other about Stefan. He wasn't an enemy of the hunters.

"You look tired, Meredith," Jack said, breaking the silence. "You doing all right?"

"I . . . I haven't been sleeping well lately," she admitted.

"Anything wrong?"

"I keep having these weird dreams," Meredith said hesitantly. It wasn't really in her nature to talk about things like this; she hated seeming weak. But she felt strangely comfortable with Jack: He was a hunter; he was like her. "I dream that I'm in a hospital room, or maybe a lab, and I can't move." Shuddering, she realized how lame her words sounded. It was hard to explain how disturbing the dreams were. "I just feel like something terrible is happening," she said weakly.

Jack nodded, his warm brown eyes sympathetic. "Sounds scary." His arm brushed Meredith's reassuringly. "But you know the dreams can't hurt you, unless you let them. They're just images your mind has created while you're asleep. It's reality we need to worry about."

"I know." And to her surprise, Meredith did feel a little better. Just bringing the dreams into the daylight, putting them into words, had made them seem harmless. Jack was right. What was scary about a few dreams when she fought monsters in real life?

inally alone, Stefan gentled his Power and sent it questing through the woods. He was aching with hunger, but he hadn't let himself feed in front of the hunters. They didn't need him rubbing their faces in the fact that they were allied with their natural enemy.

He kept his Power warm and coaxing, beckoning *come to me, come to me.* Soon he heard a light step approaching through the undergrowth. A doe stepped delicately into the clearing, her big eyes fixed on Stefan.

"Yes, that's right," he murmured. He stretched out a hand, and the doe came to him willingly, nuzzling his fingers with her soft nose. She gazed up into his eyes and gradually grew still, until the only motion in the clearing was the steady rise and fall of her flanks. Stefan lowered his face to her neck, his canines lengthening, and drank.

Long before he was satisfied, Stefan pulled away. Taking any more would leave the deer weak, and he didn't want her vulnerable to other predators because of him. "Go on," he said, slapping her lightly on the side. Shocked out of her trance, the deer started violently and leaped away, crashing through the undergrowth as she went.

Just as Stefan raised his hand to wipe the blood from his lips, his phone rang.

He fished it out of his pocket, still feeling warm from feeding, and looked at the display. *Damon.*

He let it ring again, thinking of *not* answering, but stopped himself. Katherine was dead, and whether or not that was Stefan's fault, he owed it to Damon to talk to him. Stefan had tried several times to reach Damon right after Elena had confirmed what he guessed about Katherine's death, but this was the first time his brother was returning his calls.

"Stefan." Damon's voice sounded crisply determined, as if their last conversation had never happened. "I've been following up some leads on those vampires I keep meeting up with, and I wanted—"

"Damon," Stefan broke in. "Are you all right?" He tried to put weight behind his words, knowing that Katherine's death would have changed Damon, damaged him.

And if whatever had killed Katherine was still after Damon, he was in danger. Katherine had been old and strong and clever, not an easy target. Stefan rubbed a hand across his face and leaned back against a tree, suddenly worried about his brother.

He heard Damon sigh tiredly. "I will be," he said quietly. "I've got their trail now."

"The hunted becomes the hunter," Stefan quipped, and Damon gave a short answering huff of laughter. "Damon, why did you tell Elena I wouldn't help you?" Stefan asked.

There was a pause on the other end of the line. "Because you wouldn't help me?" Damon said dryly.

"Did you *want* her to be angry with me?"

Damon was quiet for a moment, and then he exhaled, a long, weary gust of breath. "Fine," he said. "I may have not been completely fair when I spoke to Elena. Katherine's death wasn't your fault."

"I didn't know things were so bad over there," Stefan said, meeting Damon's almost-apology with one of his own.

"It's probably better that you're not here. I'd only have to protect you." There was an edge of humor in Damon's voice, and Stefan relaxed, only to feel himself tensing again at his brother's next words. "What's going on with Elena?" Damon asked. "I can feel her pushing herself, all anxious and frustrated. It's very distracting, like an itch." His tone was light, but Stefan heard real worry behind it.

Stefan sighed. His head ached, and the lingering taste of the doe's blood was suddenly sour in his mouth.

Stumbling a little over his words, he tried to explain about Trinity, about Elena's refusal to help Stefan and the hunters kill her. "I just want to protect her," he finished miserably. "Why can't Elena understand?"

There was a long silence on the other end of the phone. "Listen, little brother," Damon said finally, his voice unusually gentle. "Don't be an idiot."

"Thank you, Damon." Stefan's canines prickled with irritation. "Always a pleasure to hear from you."

"She's not a child; she's a *Guardian*, you halfwit," Damon snapped. "She loves you—how much she loves you I can feel pounding through this connection between us, even when I don't want to. She's never going to stop. But she's made to protect the innocent, and if she thinks this Trinity is one of them, then maybe you should listen to her. She might know something you don't."

Stefan felt like the wind had been knocked out of him. Had he been underestimating Elena, ignoring her instincts, so sure that he knew what was right? "I have to go," he said absently into the phone, and hung up.

Wiping the last traces of the doe's blood from his mouth with the back of his hand, he headed for home.

✳ ✳ ✳

Damon shook his head and tucked his phone back into his pocket. Stefan never had been able to take advice gracefully, not even when they'd been human. Damon had wanted to tell Stefan about Lifetime Solutions, just in case something happened, but he wasn't going to bother calling back. He'd just have to be careful.

He put the whole conversation out of his head and focused on the office building in front of him. At first glance, there was nothing special about the gray-and-glass building; it was practically designed to blend in anonymously. Only the discreet sign showing an infinity symbol and the words LIFETIME SOLUTIONS confirmed that Damon had found what he was searching for.

And it hadn't been easy to find, not at all. It had taken Damon days of searching, calling in favors, even consulting a witch, before he finally found his way here—to an inoffensive-looking office building on the outskirts of Zurich.

No legitimate business would be this hard to find—which made Damon sure that something extremely shady was going on behind these walls. Something that led straight to the seemingly unkillable vampires.

It was the end of the day, and office workers were beginning to stream from the building. Damon looked them over carefully, finally selecting a pretty young blonde who was walking alone, carrying an armful of files.

This would be easier if he was still able to use his Power to Influence anyone he wanted. Technically, the

Guardian who bound him to Elena had only forbidden him from using his Influence to *feed*, but he'd fallen out of the habit of using his Power on humans in general. Besides, they were a fickle bunch, Guardians; he didn't want to set them off.

And he still had his charm. Moving to intercept the woman, Damon bumped against her, sending her files flying to the ground.

"Oh, no," Damon said in German, "I'm so sorry. Let me help you."

The woman's face had flushed with anger, but whatever sharp reply she was about to make died on her lips once she got a good look at him. He gave her his most beguiling smile and saw her soften instantly.

By the time they'd picked up her files, Damon had learned that the woman's name was Anneli Yoder, that she was twenty-five, and that she was a secretary to a group of scientists at Lifetime Solutions.

"So, what do the scientists do in there?" he asked, his voice casual, his eyes tracing over her lips. Let her think he was asking just as an excuse to keep talking to her.

"Scientific research," Anneli said brightly, tilting her head and looking up at Damon through her long golden lashes. "Health-care stuff. Longevity is one of the things my group is working on. Some rats will live longer on a specially restricted diet, did you know that?"

"Fascinating." He carefully brushed a long golden curl back behind her ear, letting his hand linger. "I'm sure you're invaluable to your team. What do *you* do?"

"Um, I file," she said. "I take notes at the meetings and send reports to the administrators. I answer the phones."

"Interesting." Damon edged a little closer to her. Anneli's heart sped up and her lips parted unconsciously. She smelled sweet, and he regretted for a moment that he couldn't just feed on her. He was terribly hungry. "What sort of notes and reports?"

Anneli looked startled. "I don't read the reports," she said. "I just send them. And I don't really have to remember what people say in the meeting. I know stenography."

"I bet you do more than that," Damon said, his lips curling in a half smile. "Don't be modest." He was tempted to lay a touch of Power on his words, but who knew what the Guardians would take amiss? It wouldn't be worth it anyway; little Anneli didn't seem to know much.

"Well," she said, a frown creasing her smooth forehead. "I send blood samples to the lab. I have to make sure to label them correctly."

"Samples for what?" Damon asked.

Anneli blinked her big blue eyes at him. "Research."

I could have chosen a better informant, Damon thought with irritation, shooting Anneli his most blindingly bright smile. He'd chosen her because she seemed the easiest to influence without using his Power, and that apparently meant she was also the silliest woman in sight. He sent Anneli on her way, waving when she turned to shoot him an eager smile over her shoulder.

She didn't have the answers he needed. But what she did have, Damon thought with a smile, was a key card that gave her access to the building. He'd managed to slide it from her bag while they were picking up the files. With luck, Anneli wouldn't notice it was missing until tomorrow morning.

He would come back tonight and discover the secrets hidden here. Touching the key card hidden in the breast pocket of his jacket, Damon smiled.

Finally, he was on the verge of learning the secrets behind the strange vampires. The hunted would become the hunter, just like Stefan had said.

But for now he had some time to kill, and the vampires who pursued him hadn't caught up yet. Maybe he could meet someone in this city, some sweet Vittoria, and slake his hunger. Yes, Damon decided, casting one last glance at the bland office building, that was a good plan. He would come back tonight.

27

"Zander!" Bonnie objected, laughing, "I'm not tired at all. Let's go out! I want to go dancing and see everybody."

"Nope," Zander said, holding her suitcase in one hand and barring the door with the other as Bonnie tried to turn around and head out of their building. "Now that I've got you in my clutches, I want you home tonight. You have no idea how lonely I've been in our apartment, all by myself." He was grinning, but his beautiful blue eyes were serious, and Bonnie's heart gave a funny little thump.

"I missed you, too," she said, and Zander leaned down to kiss her, his mouth warm and soft against hers.

Actually, if Zander wants me all to himself tonight, I don't really have a problem with that, Bonnie decided, letting herself fall into the kiss. "I guess I can wait till tomorrow to see the others," she told him dreamily.

Zander snorted and wrapped his free arm firmly around her shoulders. "Good luck with that," he said, and swung their apartment's door open.

"Surprise!" several voices shouted. Bonnie squealed with delight and ran to throw her arms around Meredith.

"I missed you!" Bonnie shouted, and Meredith laughed, her arms tightening around her friend.

"Me, too," Meredith said. She looked tired, Bonnie noticed, dark circles under her eyes that didn't belong there, but she was smiling brightly. Alaric came up behind them and took Meredith's hand in his.

"She's been pining away since you've been gone," he remarked to Bonnie. "Once things settle down, you two need some serious girl time."

The Pack was scattered around the room, bouncing off the walls as usual: Shay and Jared enthusiastically making out in a corner of the kitchen, Camden and Marcus knocking back shots, Tristan and Spencer insulting each other, all of them wrestling, drinking, eating, making noise. Bonnie beamed at them all equally, feeling benevolent. They could be loud and wild tonight and she wouldn't care. She was just glad to be home.

"How was Chicago?" Elena asked. She kissed Bonnie on the cheek and handed her a glass of wine. "Did you get a chance to go to the Art Institute?"

"No," Bonnie said, taking a sip. "We didn't get to see a lot of the city; we were mostly working on witch stuff." She was about to elaborate on this, how they'd spent their days in meditation and herb study, their evenings in spell work, when she realized that Elena wasn't listening. Her friend's eyes were looking past her, over Bonnie's shoulder, and Bonnie turned to see what Elena was looking at.

Stefan was on the opposite side of the room, looking at Elena, his face so miserable that Bonnie's heart ached in sympathy.

Bonnie found herself holding her breath, waiting for something—she wasn't sure what—to happen. But after a second, Stefan looked away, and the moment was broken. "Well!" said Elena overbrightly, her attention switching back to Bonnie. "I'd *love* to go to the Art Institute! They have some amazing eighteenth-century paintings."

"Okay," Bonnie said tentatively. She elbowed Zander and tried to communicate *what the hell is going on with them* with a subtle eyebrow raise, but Zander only shrugged.

Bonnie turned and saw Matt for the first time—she hadn't noticed him arrive. He looked terrible, his eyes red and puffy as if he hadn't slept for days.

"Matt!" she exclaimed, and hugged him quickly. "Where's Jasmine?"

Matt flinched. "We—uh, we broke up," he said, his voice cracking.

"Oh, Matt." She laid a sympathetic hand on his arm. "What happened?" But Matt was already turning away, heading toward the kitchen.

Confused, Bonnie looked to Zander again for an explanation, but he had moved away to break up a wrestling match between Enrique and Marcus. Grabbing hold of Meredith's wrist, Bonnie dragged her to the side of the room.

"What's going on with Elena and Stefan?" she hissed as soon as they were in a private corner. "And what happened with Matt and Jasmine?" She frowned, thinking of the strained looks behind her friends' smiles, even the slightly frantic quality of the werewolves' play. "Actually, what's wrong with *everybody*?"

Meredith bit her lip.

"*Tell* me," Bonnie insisted.

"I will, I swear," Meredith said in a rush. "But tonight, can't we just be happy you're back?"

"Show us a magic trick, Bonnie!" Enrique shouted, successfully distracted from his wrestling match.

Bonnie rolled her eyes at him, then pointed a finger at Meredith. "Tomorrow," she said. "You'll tell me everything." Meredith nodded, and Bonnie walked to the center of the room, her head high. If they wanted her to have fun for one night before they told her about whatever awful things were going on, she would.

"Witch trick! Witch trick!" several of the werewolves were chanting, led by Enrique, and Bonnie smiled. Finally, she could show her friends—show Zander—what the last few weeks had been all about.

Centering herself the way she had learned in Chicago, her fingers resting against the falcon at her throat, she reached down, down, through the concrete and brick of her building to the earth beneath. Once she was planted as firmly as a tree, she stretched her consciousness *out*, and decisively grabbed on to the energy of everyone else in the room.

A shock jolted through her when she linked to Zander, and through him to the other werewolves. Their energy was rawer than she was used to, a tough, muscular power that made her quiver, feeling hyperalert. She could hear Zander's heart beating steadily next to her, could smell the sharp scent of alcohol from everyone's drinks and a sweet sticky scent coming off the cookies Elena had just brought into the room. Was this the way werewolves felt all the time?

She was more cautious linking to Stefan—his energy was powerful and dark and acutely aware. It had a colder undercurrent that made her shiver, cool and still, while the werewolves were full of life and warmth. Meredith's energy was strangely similar to Stefan's—*vampires and hunters, two sides of the same coin,* Bonnie thought, almost overwhelmed—while Alaric's felt more familiar, like that of the witches she'd worked with in Chicago. Elena's energy glowed golden and warmed Bonnie from the inside, as if her bones were gently simmering.

There was, Bonnie thought, a lot of Power here to draw on. She pulled it through herself carefully, taming the energy, and then focused it on Enrique, who was still leading the chant. Then she *shoved.*

With a startled yelp, Enrique hit the ceiling, a little harder than Bonnie had intended, and she held him there, the others' Power streaming through her.

After a moment of shocked silence, everyone, even Enrique, began to laugh.

* * *

Let's meet north of campus. 20 min?

Stefan read the text message from Jack and headed for the door. He and the lead hunter needed to talk. Jack was going to have to take Elena's Guardian instincts more seriously; they both were. Besides, it was getting late, and the party was breaking up anyway.

He sensed Elena behind him a moment before she touched his arm. "Stefan? Can I talk to you?" She looked pale and strained, her jewel-blue eyes enormous in her face.

"Yes, of course," Stefan said, his heart turning over. He'd wanted to pull her aside all evening. It had been torturous watching her, not knowing what she was thinking or how she felt about him right now. "Give me just one moment, and we'll walk home." He quickly texted Jack back *I can't tonight. Sorry*, and turned off his phone.

This was more important.

He and Elena went downstairs and out into the street together, then silently turned toward home. The night was warm and clear, stars glowing brightly overhead. The silence felt companionable, without the tension that had been hanging between him and Elena lately. After a while, Stefan's shoulders lowered, some of his anxiety leaving him. They were Elena and Stefan, and they loved each other, no matter what. He knew that. He took her hand, and she held on tightly.

"I wanted to apologize," Elena said carefully, still looking straight ahead. "Even though I don't agree with what you're doing, I know you're only trying to protect me." He admired her profile for a moment, her small nose and pointed chin, the soft swell of her lips. She looked so delicate, her skin pale and smooth in the moonlight, but he needed to remember that she wasn't.

"I'm sorry, too," he said, and she turned to look up into his face. "I know you're not helpless. You've always been strong, even before you found your Power."

He remembered that high school girl, so determined and clever and unhappy, her brave spirit holding both him and Damon spellbound, despite all their years of experience, all the women they had known. After the first shock of the similarity, it wasn't her resemblance to Katherine that had attracted them, not at all.

They had reached the door of their building. Stefan spoke hurriedly, eager to get out all the things he needed to say to her, somehow feeling that they needed to clear the air before they went inside. The next time they went home, he wanted to do it cleanly, without the strain and tension that had been hovering over them like a dark cloud.

"I've been so stubborn," Stefan said. "I know I have. I haven't been listening. Sometimes the only thing I can see is danger to you. I keep thinking, if I can just get rid of everything that threatens you, then we can be free. We can start our lives together, the lives that are going to last forever." He swallowed, suddenly finding himself very near to tears. "If I lost you, I couldn't survive it," he finished softly.

"Oh, Stefan." Elena stroked his cheek, then ran her fingers gently through his hair. "There will always be another danger. *This* is our life together. We can't waste it."

"I know," Stefan said, raising his hand to take hers. "And I should have listened to you about Trinity. I can't— I couldn't believe that she was still in there. But I believe in you. You're a Guardian and"—he had to force the words out, because so much of him was still screaming *protect Elena, save her*—"maybe you can sense something I don't." He sighed. "I trust you, Elena. If you want to try to save Trinity, I will help you."

It seemed so simple, suddenly. No matter what happened tomorrow—and he didn't know what would happen, because Trinity was dangerous and Solomon was still after Elena, none of those facts had changed—they were united again. "I love you," he told her. "More every day. We'll be together for a thousand years, longer, and I'm going to keep loving you for all of them."

Elena kissed him in answer, warm and insistent, and he pulled her even closer. They went upstairs to their apartment hand in hand, exchanging kisses the whole way.

"I have something for you," Stefan said when they were finally inside. His slow heart sped a little as he dug in his pocket for the key and put it in her hand. "It's to your house in Fell's Church," he explained, in answer to her inquiring look. "I bought it for you, from your Aunt Judith. When this is over, when Solomon is finally dead, we're going to go everywhere. I'll show you all the places I've been, and we'll find new parts of the world together. But we'll always have somewhere to come home to. We'll have a home together—your home."

Elena's eyes filled with tears. "Thank you," she whispered. "I was feeling so . . . I wasn't ready to let go of it. I want that, a home we can come back to together."

Elena is *my home*, he thought and told her so, running his fingers over the soft skin of her cheeks, her forehead, her lips, her throat, as if he could memorize her by touch. She murmured softly back to him, her breath warm, her eyes bright with life. Stefan kissed her neck, feeling her blood beating through her veins, as steady and constant as the tides.

Elena cocked her head invitingly to one side, and he gently slid his canines beneath her skin. The first mouthful of Elena's rich, warm blood brought them even closer together, two pieces of a perfect whole. *Home*, he thought again.

Elena is my home.

#TVD11StelenaForever

28

"So," Bonnie said playfully, "I couldn't help noticing a little tension between you and Stefan last night, and then this morning you're so chipper. Everything work out all right?" She waggled her eyebrows at Elena as she stirred her coffee, her spoon clinking gently against the side of the cup.

Elena could feel her cheeks heating up, which was ridiculous: She and Stefan had been living together for years. "That is a lot of pastry," she said, deflecting Bonnie's attention. "What did you do, buy out the bakery?"

They were back at Bonnie's place for breakfast, just the two of them, and Bonnie and Zander's kitchen table was heaped high with croissants, Danish, muffins, and doughnuts, as well as a big glass bowl of cut fruit and a pot of coffee.

"I know, right?" Bonnie said. "It's all Zander. It's either his way of showing how happy he is I'm home, or of making sure I get too big to get out the door again. I've never figured out if throwing all this food at me is a wolf thing or a guy thing or just a Zander thing. He's a nurturer, I guess." She stirred her coffee again and then frowned sternly at Elena. "But you're not off the hook yet. Are you and Stefan fighting?"

"I don't think it's a guy thing," Elena sidetracked. "Stefan doesn't eat and barely remembers that I do. If I didn't go to the store, there'd be nothing but blood bags and bottled water in our fridge." Bonnie shot her a look, and Elena sighed. "We're not fighting anymore. But we've still got to convince everyone else not to kill Trinity."

"I still don't understand about that. Why does everybody think Solomon is in Trinity's body?" Bonnie asked.

Elena explained. She hadn't seen Solomon—or the guy they had thought was Solomon—die, but she remembered everything Stefan and Meredith had told her, how he'd examined all of them, his intense concentration on Trinity as she'd jittered and bled. How they'd thought that Solomon was dead, but then Trinity had escaped them and turned into a powerful vampire with Solomon's yellow gaze. How the "Solomon" they'd fought wasn't originally Solomon at all, but a man named Gabriel Dalton.

Bonnie listened intently, picking at an apple turnover and asking an occasional question. When Elena finished, she shook her head, puzzled. "It doesn't sound like body-swapping to *me*," she said stubbornly.

"I forgot you were the expert on this," Elena said, with just a touch of sarcasm, and Bonnie made a face at her.

"Listen," Bonnie said. "All I've been doing this last month is working with people's energies. Everybody's got a very distinct *flavor* that's all their own."

"Like their auras," Elena said, nodding in understanding. Everyone's aura was different. "But I still haven't been able to see Solomon's aura."

"Auras, energies. Potato, po*tah*to," Bonnie said. "Just because you couldn't see it doesn't mean it wasn't there. Somehow, Solomon can shield it from you." She put down her fork and leaned forward, fixing Elena earnestly with her wide brown eyes. "My point is, if Solomon swapped bodies with Trinity, everyone would have known right away, before Solomon—or Gabriel, or whoever—died. They'd be able to tell that it wasn't the same person." Elena started to object, and Bonnie held up her hand. "Think about it," she said. "Nobody ever thought Katherine was you for more than a few minutes, even though you looked so much alike. Different energy. Similar shells, but different inside. If the people who knew her thought it was still Trinity in there—and they hunted with her, they must know her really well—then it *was* Trinity."

"But when Meredith saw her, she was a vampire," Elena said helplessly. "And she had Solomon's eyes. Do you think she's possessed? That was Alaric's other theory."

"I'm pretty sure you have to be a demon to possess somebody," Bonnie said dismissively. "Old Ones aren't demons; they're just really powerful, ancient vampires." She went back to picking at her turnover, frowning thoughtfully. "I think I know what it is, though," she said.

Elena stared at her. "Go on."

Bonnie rested her elbows on the table and cupped her chin in her hands. "I can do a lot of things now that I couldn't do before, some of them by drawing on other people's energy, like I did last night." Elena nodded. She'd felt Bonnie tugging at her, knew she had somehow used Elena's own Power to levitate Enrique. "And if I were a bad person, a really Powerful one"—Bonnie looked at Elena— "like an Old One, I think I could go the other way."

"What do you mean?" Elena asked.

"If I were strong enough, I could take my own energy and force it *into* someone else instead of using their energy. I could fill them up with myself and make them do whatever I wanted. It would just be flipping the switch the other way, really."

"That sounds like possession," Elena said, confused, but Bonnie shook her head impatiently.

"No," she explained. "In possession, the demon is actually going inside the person and taking their body for their own. This would be more like a really powerful kind of compulsion. Solomon isn't *inside* Trinity; he's just *using* her. Since he's so strong, he could transfer his own attributes—like the yellow eyes, and being a vampire—but she's just compelled. She's still there, underneath all this Power he's forcing into her."

Hope bloomed in Elena's chest. This was scary stuff, but it was also the first real suggestion that saving Trinity was a viable plan. "So you're saying Solomon *does* have a body, still out there somewhere," she said breathlessly. "We've been hunting the wrong targets all along—first Gabriel, and then Trinity—while the right one, the real Solomon, has stayed hidden."

Bonnie grinned and jumped up from the table, rattling the plates. She held her hand out to Elena. "Come on," she said impatiently. "If you've been looking for the wrong people all this time, maybe it's time to start trying to find the right one."

In the bedroom, Bonnie spread out a map out over the king-size bed. "This is the whole state," she told Elena. "This kind of compulsion must take a lot of Power. I don't think he could do it from somewhere farther away." She placed a purple candle on each post of the bed, carefully, then lit them all. "Purple's good for divination and psychic stuff," she explained.

She stepped across from Elena, the bed and the map between them, and stretched out her hands. "I need you to use your Guardian Power," she told her.

Elena shook her head. "It doesn't work on Solomon," she said. "I've been searching and searching for him. I couldn't find Gabriel or Trinity, either. There's no trace of them."

"Like I said, he must be able to shield himself from you somehow," Bonnie said. "He knows that you can find evil and is doing something to protect himself from you." She grinned mischievously, her teeth white in the candlelight. "But he doesn't know what *I* can do. Trust me."

And Elena did. She reached for Bonnie's hands, then, shutting her eyes for a moment, felt for her Power. She thought of the evil Solomon had done: taking over Trinity and the unknown Gabriel Dalton; killing gentle Andrés, his blood flowing red across the bed; poor little broken Sammy.

When she opened her eyes, Elena could see Bonnie's aura, gentle and rosy pink all around her, and her own golden one next to it, but there was no trace of evil, nothing for her to follow. "You see the problem," she said.

"Just wait," Bonnie told her. She began to mutter words in some ancient language, and the candle flames stretched higher, flickered wildly, although there was no breeze. The little hairs on Elena's arms prickled.

Then, Bonnie's aura was mixing with her own, the rose and the gold looking like the shifting colors of a summer dawn. At the same time, Elena felt a gentle, insistent tugging somewhere near her collarbone—Bonnie asking *let me in, let me in*. Gulping nervously, she tried to open herself and let Bonnie take what she needed.

Bonnie spoke faster, the ancient words tumbling over one another in a low monotone, and then, suddenly, she fell silent. From each candle a golden ray arced over Bonnie and Elena, over the bed, to meet above the map. A single point of flame fell, scorching the map. And then the candles flickered out.

"There," Bonnie said, laying her finger on the scorch mark. "It worked."

Elena stared numbly. "We've been looking in the wrong places all along," she whispered. "Solomon's not even in Dalcrest."

29

After more than five hundred years, Stefan didn't think he should be afraid of the dark, but something about this place unnerved him. They were deep underground in an old reservoir— water hadn't been stored here for years, but the stone was still damp and clammy, moss spotting its surface. Dim light filtered down from above, just enough to navigate by.

"It's like some kind of pagan underworld," Alaric said, wonderingly.

Stefan smiled weakly in acknowledgment but didn't reply. It was so quiet here, just the soft sound of their footsteps and a steady drip of water, somewhere out in the dark. The heavy graveyard scent of the wet stone overlaid everything, and the echo distorted sound, making it impossible for Stefan to tell if there were any noises or smells that didn't belong.

The werewolves didn't like it. They were interspersed among the humans, whining softly in protest, their tails down and their ears back unhappily. Bonnie, striding along just behind Elena, had her hand on Zander's back, her fingers twined in his thick white fur. Stefan wasn't sure who was reassuring whom.

This was Bonnie and Elena's mission, and Stefan hoped that they were right, that Solomon was here somewhere, not in Trinity's body back in Dalcrest. The tightness in Jack's face said that he was taking a lot on faith and wasn't happy about it. "Every moment that we waste here, Trinity could be murdering innocent people," he muttered to Meredith under his breath, but Stefan, with his sharp vampiric senses, heard him.

When Elena had told him that she and Bonnie believed they knew where the real Solomon was hidden—in an abandoned underground reservoir outside a small town called Stag's Crossing, about forty miles from Dalcrest— Stefan had hesitated.

But now, watching brave, beautiful Elena following a trail only she could see, Stefan had faith in her. Elena always came through.

It was getting colder, he realized suddenly. Frost crunched under his heels. Meredith, usually so sure-footed, slipped and swore as she struggled to regain her balance.

The wolves drew closer to the humans, and Tristan let out an uneasy whine.

They rounded a corner, and something moved ahead of them in the dim light. Matt flicked up his crossbow and shot without hesitating.

The crossbow bolt stopped in midair and clattered to the ground.

Stefan tried to leap forward and found that, just like at the Plantation Museum, his muscles refused to obey him. The others in front of him were equally still, Zander frozen with one paw raised, Bonnie in the act of turning her head to look toward Elena.

Solomon stepped out of the darkness.

He was not, Stefan thought with a shock of surprise, particularly impressive. At first glance, he was a small, almost timid-looking man, the type of person you might pass on the street without a second look. Nothing like handsome Gabriel Dalton or tall, sweet-faced Trinity. His light brown hair straggled down past his ears, and his shoulders were hunched. Were it not for the Power that held them all helpless, Solomon would have been easy to underestimate.

Then he looked up and his eyes flashed golden in the darkness, and Stefan knew this was him. Those eyes were full of cold intelligence and pure malice, the eyes of something slimy and primeval that had watched from under a rock for countless millennia as civilizations rose and fell.

Solomon stepped closer to them, closer to Elena, and Stefan went cold with dread.

His worst fears were being realized, and there was nothing Stefan could do about it. He couldn't move. He couldn't speak. He could barely breathe. All he could do was watch as everything that mattered to him was about to be destroyed.

"A pretty girl," Solomon said, his voice dry and rasping, and reached a hand out to touch Elena's face.

Stefan wanted to scream with rage, wanted to strike Solomon and knock him back, but no matter how hard he tried, he couldn't move.

Almost gently, Solomon traced a finger over Elena's cheekbones, over her soft lips, across her delicate chin. And everywhere he touched, Elena began to bleed, tiny droplets coming through her skin and running down the surface of her face. Stefan could smell the richness of Elena's blood everywhere, and his canines throbbed and lengthened against his will.

"Lovely," Solomon said approvingly. He stroked his fingers through Elena's blood, smearing it in feathery patterns across her face. "Perfect."

There were footsteps coming toward them, and Solomon looked up, his golden eyes sharp. Stefan's hopes rose for a second. Maybe this was someone who could help them.

"There you are," Solomon said approvingly, and Stefan's heart sank again. Even though he couldn't see her yet, he knew who it was. Trinity. Whatever was left of her, fully in thrall to this wicked Old One.

Please, not Elena. Let her live, he prayed to the God he had believed in unquestioningly as a human. A stream of blood ran down Elena's chin, dripping to stain her shirt. She was terribly pale.

Beyond Elena, he could see Solomon, his golden eyes following Trinity. She hesitated directly behind Stefan, then passed him by. A moment later there was the sound of skin striking skin and a steady trickle of liquid hitting the stone floor. *Blood*, Stefan realized with horror, smelling the coppery, rich scent. Trinity had hurt someone, but he didn't know who.

Solomon smiled. "Come here," he ordered.

Trinity walked straight to Solomon and stood before him, her hands folded in front of her and her face upturned to his in a parody of an obedient child. Golden eyes gazed into golden eyes, and Solomon's smile broadened.

"Hunters," he said slowly. "Your old friends. Which shall we kill first?" He looked from one side of the group to the other, slowly, and then nodded. "Jack, of course." His gaze narrowed on the hunter, next to Stefan. "I don't trust him."

Trinity came back toward them, her shoulder brushing Stefan's as she stretched to reach Jack's throat. She gave a soft sound of satisfaction as her teeth pierced his vein. Stefan could smell her now. She stank revoltingly of old blood and sweat.

Solomon stretched out a hand toward Elena again, his fingernails long and black with filth. Tracing one across Elena's collarbone, he sighed theatrically. "So pretty," he said again. "I'd like to keep you, little Guardian, make you mine." Where his finger traced, Elena's skin split open, blood pouring out over her collarbone, down across her chest, staining her shirt with gore. "Sadly, though, I think I should get rid of you now. Your blood is too much a danger to me," Solomon finished quietly.

Staring helplessly straight ahead, Stefan wanted to die. He would gladly die, if it would protect Elena.

Elena's arm quivered.

At first Stefan thought it was an illusion of the dim, wavery light. But then Bonnie blinked, a slow, definite blink. They were still touching, he realized. They were working together, in the same way that they had managed to work together to locate Solomon.

Elena's eyes flicked to meet Stefan's, clear, brilliant blue despite the blood running down her face. In them he could read her message: *Be ready.*

It was so cold that the first touch of warmth spreading inside him felt like fire. He knew without questioning that it came from Elena.

Trinity was feeding from Jack beside him, making thick slurping noises. Solomon glanced away from Elena for a moment, watching whatever horror his puppet was perpetrating, and then turned his gaze back to her, drawing a knife from a sheath at his waist. Stefan recognized it: It had once been Trinity's. A hunter's knife.

The burning warmth filled his body. Stefan knew he would only get this one chance, and that only if he were very lucky. Solomon pressed the knife slowly against Elena's throat. Suddenly, Stefan sucked in a breath, all his muscles screaming in protest as he forced them to move at once. Lunging forward with a massive effort, Stefan raised his machete and brought it across Solomon's neck.

Solomon's body fell slowly and as it landed, the ice beneath him cracked. For a long moment, everything was silent. Then Trinity fell backward to the ground and began to sob.

Stefan couldn't look away from Solomon, a small skinny body on the cold stone floor. He looked so inconsequential. How many people had he sent out to the world to dance at his command? Jack had been right: Solomon left no trace, because he didn't need to be there to destroy.

When Stefan finally tore his eyes away, he saw that Trinity was kneeling next to Jack, his head cradled in her hands. "I'm so sorry," she sobbed, her eyes their normal, untroubled blue. "Oh, my God. I don't . . . it's all like a dream. A nightmare."

"It's okay, Trinity," Jack reassured her. Blood was still streaming from the bite on his neck, but he wiped it away. "It's all going to be all right."

And then Elena was in Stefan's arms, whispering, "We did it, we did it," kissing his face and holding him so tight he thought she might never let him go. The open cut on her collarbone was barely beginning to clot. Stefan automatically bit his own wrist and held it out for her.

"Drink," he said. She bent to suck at his wrist, and he watched her affectionately. "*You* did it," he told her. "You and Bonnie." He could feel the glorious, thankful strength of Elena, and he lost himself in it, feeling his own triumph and relief echoed back to him.

We're free at last, he told her silently. *We can finally live in peace.*

#TVD11StakingSolomon

30

Now here, Damon thought smugly, *is the good stuff.*

It had taken awhile to find it. At first, Lifetime Solutions' offices seemed disappointingly reputable. There was a room full of caged lab rats, none of them growing fangs or second heads. The notes on their treatments were incomprehensible to Damon, just lists of experimental medications and reactions in highly technical jargon. The papers in the filing cabinets were similarly dull, and he hadn't been able to bypass the passwords to investigate the computers properly.

Everything seemed boringly, incomprehensibly normal. If Damon hadn't found a business card from this company in the pocket of one of those strange vampires, he would have dismissed it as completely ordinary.

Now he was standing in what was clearly the CEO's office. Bigger and more richly furnished than any of the others, with wide floor-to-ceiling windows and a large seating area. Damon had gone through the desk drawers, the cabinets at one side of the room, the coat closet in the corner. Nothing.

Nothing except that the top drawer of the desk seemed shallower than it ought to be. Damon jiggled it, then carefully tilted the drawer back and slid it forward. Just as he'd thought, there was a small keyhole at the top of the back of the drawer. A secret, locked compartment. Interesting.

The lock wasn't much of a challenge; lock picking was a skill Damon had learned centuries ago. Inside the compartment was a thick notebook bound in brown leather.

Damon quickly flipped through the pages, growing ever more curious. It seemed to be some kind of journal: part philosophical musings, part the record of a series of experiments.

There must be a way to improve with science what can be imperfectly wrought by magic, Damon read. *My subjects begin to develop, then die without warning, their hearts bursting under their new stresses. Is there a way to strengthen the circulatory system and allow improved capacity? Multiple surgeries will be necessary.*

Subject K4 showed promise, but the side effects of the adrenaline and stimulants were too great. Subject proved ungovernable and prone to uncontrollable fits of rage. After dismemberment of lab assistant, subject was destroyed.

"Subject K4 didn't want to bow down to you, did he, Doctor?" Damon muttered. The back of his neck was prickling uneasily as he read: There was something very, very wrong here. He flipped forward a few pages and read on.

After the deaths of the first batch of test subjects and the disaster of Subject K4, the doctor had adjusted the dosages and streamlined a course of surgeries, not just on the circulatory system but on the muscles, digestive system, brain, and even facial structure and teeth.

And, gradually, his experiments began to survive.

A high dose of iron and protein is necessary to combat the anemia that results from the new bone density. Is the traditional blood diet less mystical and more practical than previously thought?

Blood diet. Damon suddenly realized what he was reading. This person was trying to *make* vampires.

Trying, and apparently succeeding. As the doctor fine-tuned the surgeries and medications for his experiments, the pages Damon was reading became a record of triumphs.

As I had suspected, there is no reason but mysticism for the limitations of the natural vampire. By rerouting the circulatory system and adding a large dose of melanin to the initial medication, I have made my subjects impervious to the traditional methods of controlling their population: Subjects can walk easily in the sun and are not harmed by wood to the heart.

Nonphysical methods of identification proved more difficult at first to bypass. Test subjects were readily identified as unnatural by humans with highly developed senses: so-called "psychics" and "seers."

Auras, Damon thought. *He's talking about people who can read auras, like Elena.* The doctor had eventually found a way around this, too. Through intensive meditation and a high dosage of serotonin inhibitors, the lab-created vampires had managed to learn to hide or disguise their auras.

This, Damon thought, absently tapping the page with one finger, *could be useful.* He read on.

Finally, after so many trials and errors, the experiment has been an unqualified success. My subjects have all the advantages of the natural vampire: They do not appear to age or contract illnesses, they are stronger and faster than humans, they have highly developed senses. And yet I have been able to circumvent the disadvantages that keep natural vampires from being the perfect predators: Unlike their wild cousins, my subjects are not endangered by wood or sunlight. The time has come to move on to Stage B of the experiment.

Stage B? Damon flipped forward again and blinked in surprise at what he found. In the next stage of his experiment, the doctor had used the technique on himself. It made sense, Damon supposed. Certainly if he had created the ultimate predator, he wouldn't want to remain prey.

This didn't really explain why the doctor's lab-manu-factured vampires had been coming after Damon, though. He kept reading.

To take dominance in the natural world, it is necessary to eliminate competitive species. The vampire has survived unchanged for too long; in some cases for thousands of years. These targets must be eliminated for my bold new world to be possible. The greatest threat to my new creations is their inspira-tion: the traditional vampire.

Turning one more page, Damon found two lists of names.

The first was Old Ones, he recognized immedi-ately. First names only—the Old Ones came from a time before people needed more than one name. *Klaus, Celine, Benevenuto, Alexander*—Old Ones he knew Stefan and his friends had killed, each one crossed out in black ink. Other names he didn't recognize—*Chihiro, Gunnar of the North, Milimo, Pachacuti*—were crossed out in red.

Only one name remained unmarked: *Solomon.*

"You've been busy, Doctor Jekyll," Damon muttered, tracing over the red-crossed names with one finger.

The second list was much longer—and much worse. Many of these crossed-out names were vampires Damon knew.

Anne Grimmsdotir: a quiet, fierce girl who had wan-dered the North since the days of the Vikings. She didn't talk much, but she was graceful and quick.

Sophia Alexiou: beautiful, elegant Sophia, whom Damon had spent a Mediterranean winter with once, more than a century ago.

Abioye Ogunwale: Sharp-tongued and stubborn, he'd always been a gambler. He'd won Damon's favorite boots in a card game, back in the seventeenth century.

Damon stared at the names, an uncomfortable tightness growing in his chest. They hadn't been friends, these vampires—Damon didn't really make friends—but they were people Damon had met again and again over the course of a very long life. Old vampires, strong vampires, who'd hunted and traveled and survived for centuries. All of them *murdered* for a bold new world of man-made vampires?

Halfway down the page was written: *Katherine von Swartzschild*. It hadn't been crossed out yet. "Behind the times, Doctor," Damon said softly, feeling a pang in his chest at the sight of her name.

At the bottom of the page, the last names on the list: *Damon Salvatore. Stefan Salvatore. Dalcrest, Virginia.*

Damon placed his hand flat on the book and took a breath, thinking hard.

There were very few people in the world about whom he gave a damn. Now that Katherine was dead, that list was pretty much limited to Elena and Stefan. If pushed, he might admit to a sentimental fondness for his little redbird

Bonnie, and a grudging respect for Meredith, the hunter. And every single one of these people was in Dalcrest, Virginia.

Damon stuffed the book into the front of his coat pocket and slipped out of the lab, as silent as a shadow, almost as if he were already becoming a ghost.

#TVD11TVDsMostWanted

* * *

"A toast!" Alaric said, raising his glass high. "To the end of the Old Ones!" Everyone clinked their glasses as a wave of giddy laughter flooded Elena and Stefan's apartment. Wrapping her fingers around the stem of her wineglass, Elena looked around and smiled at their gathered friends.

It was hard to believe that a few hours ago they'd been in the dim, cold underground, unable to move. Elena had been so sure it was the end for all of them.

And then, in the midst of the cold, she'd felt a tiny spark of warmth. Bonnie's hand, where it touched her arm, was the only warm thing in the whole world. *I'm here, Elena*, she heard Bonnie say into her mind. *Let me in.* Focusing all her energy on that one spot, Elena had sent Power to Bonnie in a steady, thin stream. And Bonnie had freed Stefan.

Stefan's arms wrapped around her from behind, jarring her from the unsettling memory. He kissed her neck lightly, then laughed, more relaxed than Elena had seen him in a long, long time. *We're free*, he told her silently whenever their lips touched, *we're free. You're safe.*

Tomorrow they would make plans—head out to Europe to find Damon, and make sure he was safe. Then together they would wander Europe, all of it, the cobblestone streets of Stefan's past and the tall, glass cities of the modern age. *Paris*, Elena thought, remembering the time she had been there in high school, before she even met Stefan. It felt like a lifetime ago. She couldn't wait to go back and see it all again, with Stefan by her side.

Tomorrow they would begin the rest of their endless lives. But for now they were with their friends, and Elena was happy.

Even Trinity was with them, looking pale and thin, but alive.

Jack stood, and Trinity looked up at him, her gaze full of hero worship. *I wonder if he'll tell her he was planning to kill her*, part of Elena wondered, somewhat cynically.

Jack smiled widely and warmly around at them all. He was using his hunter's stave like a walking stick, resting his weight on it lightly. "To unlikely allies and unexpected friends," he said, raising his glass.

Elena joined in the toast and then felt her phone vibrate. She paused to discreetly fish it out of her bag and glance at the screen. It was a voice mail from Damon. Tentatively, she poked at the connection between them, and almost recoiled at the anxiety pulsing through their bond.

Before she could slip quietly out of the room, Jack walked over to her and Stefan, blocking her exit. "Stefan, you've been a huge help in this hunt," he said. Elena nudged Stefan with her foot, and they exchanged a private smile. She was pretty sure that Stefan had ended up *leading* the hunt, not just helping with it.

"I can't thank you enough," Stefan told Jack solemnly. "To know that all the threats we've been chasing for so long are gone at last. Elena and I are so happy."

"*Almost* all the threats," Jack said thoughtfully, and Elena's head snapped up at the new, darker tone in his voice. And then she saw, panicking, that Jack's aura was *wrong*. Rusty red, the color of dried blood, was running through the familiar warm brown, spreading like a web of veins. Elena opened her mouth to shout a warning, but she was too late.

Baring his teeth to show his elongated canines— *and how could he be a vampire, Elena would have known, Stefan would have known*—Jack moved, faster and smoother than Elena would have believed possible, and slammed his stave cleanly through Stefan's chest. Stefan gasped, a long, rattling gasp, then fell heavily to the floor. Jack ran out the door before Elena could even scream.

Elena fell to her knees as the room erupted into chaos around her. Alaric laid a hand on the stave to pull it from Stefan's chest but Meredith stopped him. "Pulling it out won't help," she said. "If it's still there, it might give him more time."

Elena only had eyes for Stefan, but he was blurry through her tears. "Hold on, Stefan," she said desperately, stroking his face. He muttered something and scrabbled at her arm, his fingers weak. "Bonnie!" Elena screamed. "Bonnie, can't you fix—?" Bonnie dropped to her knees beside them, her face white, but shook her head.

"I'm sorry, I'm sorry, I don't think there's a spell for this—" she said frantically.

Elena reached for her Guardian Power and sent its golden light racing through Stefan, trying to heal what was broken. But the dark and cold radiating from the stake in his heart swallowed up the light as fast as she could feed it to him. He was sinking; she could feel it. He was slipping away.

* * *

Stefan's eyes were glazing over, and his grip on Elena's arm loosened. "No, no!" Elena was yelling, grabbing at him, trying to keep him with her. "*Please*, Stefan."

Tears were dripping off her face onto Stefan's, running over his pale cheeks. *No, no, no*, Elena's mind babbled frantically. *Not like this; we're supposed to have forever together. Please. Please.*

Stefan's eyes were moving beneath his lids, flicking from side to side. His breath rattled in his chest. His face was tight, almost fearful. Elena took his hand in hers and pressed her lips to his.

Her mind and Stefan's touched, the instant connection between them as strong as ever, and she wrapped him in her consciousness, trying to hold him, to keep him safe. She would never let him be afraid, not if she could help it.

But darkness and emptiness were spreading through him. *Stefan, my love, my darling,* she thought, *please.* That was all she could think of, protestations of love, pet names, and the single word *please. Please stay with me, my darling one. Hang on. I love you.* Her tears fell against his cold face, her lips warm against his cold ones.

Elena? His mind reached out for hers. He was disoriented, and she clung to him, trying to reassure him. *It's all right,* she thought desperately. *It'll all be okay.*

You can't save me, Elena. Stefan's thought was terribly sad, but there was no trace of fear in it. *I'm so sorry. I thought we'd be safe. I thought we'd have our whole, long lives together. I wish there were time.*

No! Don't go, Elena thought, pleading, frantic. *Please, I can't let you go.*

I don't want to. But be happy without me. Promise me you'll find a way to be happy.

Elena couldn't imagine ever being happy again. *I promise,* she thought, tears running down her face.

Believe in yourself. Trust your friends. He sounded terribly tired, but there was a warmth in his thoughts that felt like a smile. *Never forget how much I love you. You deserve to be loved.*

Elena choked back a sob. *Stefan, you're the love of my life. My whole life.* His consciousness brushed against hers like a caress.

The darkness that had infected Stefan rolled on, taking over more and more of him, as unstoppable as a tide. Elena held onto him, sending more of her Power through him, but the darkness swallowed it like a black hole, swallowed everything, until she was just lying with her arms around him, murmuring, *Stefan, I love you, I love you, please . . .*

The dark tide rolled out, and took Stefan with it.

#TVD11RIP

31

"**I** gave Elena valerian and some other sedative herbs and sat with her until she fell asleep," Bonnie said, coming out of the bedroom. "She couldn't stop crying, but eventually she just passed out."

She had felt so helpless, watching Elena lying there, tears slipping silently from her closed eyes and down her cheeks, looking small in the bed she'd shared with Stefan.

Tears flooded Bonnie's eyes. Stefan had been so strong, the calm at the center of the storm, and he and Elena had been the focus of their group, the ones the others all revolved around. She couldn't quite comprehend him being *dead*.

Meredith and Matt were seated on the sofa in the living room, looking as broken as Bonnie felt. Bonnie went over to them with a sigh, pulling her feet under her on the sofa and curling up next to Meredith. Zander was with most of the Pack, combing the woods in search of Jack, while Alaric was researching, trying to find what kind of vampire could hide his aura like Jack had. Trinity, Darlene, and Alex had returned to their motel, where four of the Pack watched over them, just in case. But the remaining hunters had seemed as shocked as the others that Jack was a vampire. Bonnie remembered that Jack wasn't really one of them, that he had come to this group and enlisted them in his quest to kill Solomon.

Bonnie was glad the others were somewhere else. It felt right to watch over Elena with just Matt and Meredith, the four friends who had gone through so much together, who had known one another longest of all.

"I just don't understand it," Matt murmured, twisting his hands together miserably. "How did we not know Jack was a vampire? And why would he kill Stefan? They'd been working together. They were *friends*."

"He walked in the daylight, without a ring," Meredith said dully. "He was obsessed with killing vampires. He was a hunter. But he was a vampire, too?"

Matt cleared his throat. When they looked at him, he straightened his shoulders and said, with an obvious effort, "We should call Damon."

Meredith and Bonnie stared at each other in dismay. How could they have forgotten Damon? Despite all the years of conflict between the brothers, Bonnie was certain that Stefan's death would tear Damon apart. And an angry, grieving Damon might do anything.

She could see that Meredith was having the same thoughts.

"Elena should tell him," Meredith said.

Matt frowned. "Elena's got enough on her plate. We need to make things easier for her."

Bonnie shook her head decisively, her red curls flying around her. "Elena's the only one who can keep Damon from totally losing it. And she'll probably *want* to tell him. We should wait till morning anyway, and talk to her about it then."

"I guess you're right," Matt said. "I just—all I want to do is help her."

"We all do," Bonnie said, taking Matt's broad hand in her smaller one. "But I think the only thing we can do now is be here if she needs us."

Matt rubbed a tired hand over his eyes. "I still can't believe it," he said. "I can't . . . I never thought I'd see Stefan fall like that. Any of us, I worried about, but I thought he'd go on forever."

Bonnie buried her face in Matt's shoulder and, even though she'd promised herself she'd be strong, felt a few tears squeeze out of her eyes. "Let's stay here tonight," she said, her voice muffled in his shirt. "Elena shouldn't be alone."

"The sofa folds out," Meredith said, jumping up, glad of something practical to do. "And I think there's an air mattress in the closet."

They got ready for bed quietly. Bonnie climbed into the sofa bed next to Meredith and turned out the light. Listening to Meredith's breathing next to her and Matt's from the floor by the bed, she knew that neither of them was going to fall asleep tonight either.

They would lie here together, in the long dark hours before dawn, watching over Elena. It was the only thing they could do.

* * *

In the pitch-blackness, Elena's eyes flew open. She didn't know how much time had passed since she drank Bonnie's potion, but it had put her into a deep, dreamless sleep.

And now she was awake, and something was scratching at the window.

She was just drawing breath to scream when she realized that of course she knew who it was. She could feel him. Slipping out of bed, Elena fumbled her way toward the window, banging her leg against her bureau in the dark.

Damon was sitting on a tree branch outside, his inscrutable black eyes fixed on her. "Invite me in, princess," he said.

"Come in," Elena said, and stumbled back from the window as Damon stepped inside, as graceful as ever. When he wrapped his arm around her shoulders, she realized he was shaking.

She didn't need to tell him anything, she realized, somewhat gratefully. He already knew, must have known as soon as he'd felt her anguish. His heartache came steadily through the bond between them, mirroring hers.

"I need . . ." he said, his voice broken. "Can I hold you?" She nodded wordlessly.

On top of the covers, he held her loosely, his arms strong and comforting. Elena rested her head against his chest and finally let go, knowing that the link between them made words unnecessary, his pain and her pain blending until it was all one shared emotion. Sobbing, she wiped a hand roughly under her nose. She was gross and covered with snot and tears and she didn't care.

"Stefan would have liked to have seen you again," she told Damon in a thick, tear-choked voice. "He missed you while you were gone."

"I know. I missed him, too," Damon said, and their bond throbbed with an extra ache: loneliness, and regret over time lost. He stroked her hair with a heavy, comforting hand.

Elena pressed her face against his chest. Damon, she realized, was the only person in the world who understood exactly what she had lost. She held onto him fiercely as they grieved together, weeping for Stefan and for themselves.

#TVD11DamonReturns

32

The sun was so bright Matt had to shield his eyes as he came up to his apartment building. It had been a long, terrible night. Whenever he started to fall into sleep, he had remembered Stefan, a stave in his chest and a terrible emptiness in his eyes, falling like a broken doll. Remembered Elena's screams. Stefan's blood had dried on his sleeve.

Stefan, his friend. Once his rival for Elena's affection—although it had never been much of a contest—briefly his football teammate, his ally against the darkness. Gone. Matt should have sensed that something was wrong about Jack. He should have protected his friends.

Jasmine was standing outside the front door of his building. Seeing her in the glaring sunshine gave Matt a weird sense of déjà vu, as if he had fallen through a wormhole and ended up back at that terrible morning when she had told him good-bye.

"What do you want?" he asked her, his voice flat. He didn't want to be rude—Jasmine had every right to have left him—but he was so tired. He couldn't handle anything more today.

"I miss you," Jasmine said, her words rushed. She looked up at him with big, appealing eyes, a tiny nervous smile tilting up the corners of her mouth. "I miss you so much, Matt. Can't we try again?"

Matt felt as if he was dissolving, falling into a million pieces. He wanted that so badly. Warm, loving, beautiful Jasmine. She healed people, and even though she saw so much that was terrible—every doctor did—she stayed innocent; she was *good* all the way through.

"I can't," he said roughly. "Nothing's changed, Jasmine. No, things have gotten *worse*." He brandished his spattered sleeve at her. "See that? It's Stefan's blood; Stefan is *dead*."

Ignoring her soft, pained gasp, he went on. "Everything's dark and scary and awful, but I still can't turn my back on my friends. I can't ignore the darkness." His eyes burned, and he hunched in on himself. "I'm not someone you can plan a future with," he said softly.

Jasmine reached out for Matt, her warm hands taking hold of his arms, covering the bloodstains. She wasn't turning away, he realized.

"Do you know why I came here today?" she asked, and Matt shrugged miserably. "A couple was brought in last night from a horrible car accident." She squeezed her eyes tightly shut just for a moment, as if she was blocking out the memory.

"Even though they were both so badly hurt and in so much pain," she went on, "they were reaching out for each other's hands. They were so worried about each other." She looked at Matt, naked pleading in her eyes. "Bad things happen every day, just driving down the highway. And when they happen, I don't want to be miles away from you. I want to be able to reach out for your hand."

Matt started to speak again—God, yes, he wanted that, but how could he expect her to share this life?—and Jasmine put a hand over his mouth to shush him. "What you and your friends do, fighting monsters so that people like me, can live normal, happy lives? It's so important. You kept who you really are a secret from me, and I understand why. But I want to know now. Matt, I want to be part of this. Please give me another chance."

She swallowed hard and looked to him anxiously, her eyes bright with tears. Matt couldn't even think. He just moved instinctively forward, taking Jasmine in his arms, resting his cheek against her head, smelling the sweet scent of her shampoo.

Jasmine had come back to him—and maybe, somehow, they would get through this dark time together.

*   *   *

Alaric and Zander had dug a grave down by the river, not far from the charred remains of the Plantation Museum. It was a lonely looking band who stood around it, Damon thought: Bonnie, his little redbird, clinging hard to the arm of her wolf boy; hunter Meredith looking bruised and wary, her hand tight in the hand of her scholar husband. Sturdy Matt, his head bowed and his eyes red, a girl Damon didn't know standing quietly beside him.

And Elena, silent and withdrawn, the wind whipping her long blond hair around her shoulders. She was staring at nothing, her face swollen and tear-streaked.

Even like this, ravaged with grief, she was still beautiful, Damon thought. His gut tightened. How many times had he thought *If only Stefan were out of the way?* And now Stefan was gone and it was wrong, all wrong.

They'd wrapped Stefan's body in white silk and laid him carefully in the grave, his weapons around him. It was a beautiful spot they'd chosen, the river flowing past with a continual soothing sound of rushing water, moss-covered tree trunks rising up around them. A breeze fluttered the corner of the silk, its motion a parody of life, and Damon gritted his teeth. Everyone was waiting for someone else to begin Stefan's last rites.

Picking up a handful of dirt from the pile by the grave, he walked to the edge and let it trickle slowly from his fingers over Stefan's body, dark earth sullying the clean white cloth. "It's a waste," he said, his voice hard and vicious to his own ears. "Stefan tried so hard; he worked and *worked* to not be a vampire, to fight who he had become. And he died still hating what he was." Damon opened his hand, letting the rest of the dirt spill into the grave.

They were looking at him with pity in their eyes, all of them, and Damon was suddenly furious. He didn't need their pity; he could destroy them with a touch, pull down this little town around them. He could fly away, leave them behind, and never look back.

But he could feel Elena's dull grief through the bond between them, and so he put out a hand to touch her arm, and stayed.

Bonnie stepped forward next. "Stefan was so brave," she said. "Even when Elena d-died"—she threw a look of panic at the others—"even when things were so bad for him, he came when I called him for help. He was a really good friend. He loved Elena and he tried to protect all of us. He *saved* us all, more than once." Her lip was wobbling dangerously, and Zander stepped up next to her, touching her arm in reassurance. "I don't want him to be alone," she went on, her voice thin and high. Taking a small white silk bag from her pocket, she held it over the grave. "This is filled with rosemary and sweet peas, for friendship, and remembrance. I won't forget Stefan." Bonnie let the silk bag fall into the grave, then took a handful of dirt and dropped it in.

"Werewolves and vampires are enemies," Zander said, staring down at Stefan's body, "but Stefan taught me that it's not so simple. He was a friend to the Pack." He dropped a handful of dirt into the grave, too, and he and Bonnie stepped back together, Bonnie leaning on him for support.

Meredith let her handful of dirt fall into the grave and gazed down at Stefan's body. "Stefan was good and strong, and he'd just defeated the last of the vampires he'd hunted for years," she said. "He was happy. When I fight now, when I'm hunting the monsters that Stefan and I hunted together, I'll be fighting for him, too." She took a stake from her belt. "Stefan carved this," she said. "He hunted with it. He should have it." She dropped the stake in, and they all heard the soft thump as it hit the bottom of the grave.

As she turned away, Alaric stepped forward and looked to Damon. "I know they would have said a mass for the dead in Latin, when you and Stefan were young," he said hesitantly. "Even though he didn't go to church anymore,

I thought maybe Stefan would have liked . . ." He gestured shyly at the piece of paper clutched in one hand.

Damon shrugged. Maybe Stefan would have liked it; he didn't know. He was sure, though, that his brother would have listened politely to whatever Alaric planned to read.

Alaric unfolded the paper and began, "*Inclina, Domine, aurem tuam ad preces nostras quibus misericordiam tuam supplices deprecamur; ut animam famuli tui . . .*" *Incline thy ear, O Lord, to the prayers with which we entreat Thy mercy, and in a place of peace and rest, establish the soul of Thy servant . . .*

Damon felt his lips twist in a bitter smile at the familiar words. Alaric's accent was terrible. Even in the universities they didn't teach proper Latin anymore. And Damon was fairly certain that the fierce God he and Stefan had worshipped in their childhood would have no place of peace and rest for vampires. The Guardians had said, he remembered, that when a vampire died, he simply ceased to exist. Still, if the prayer comforted these children, let them have it.

Alaric finished reading the prayer, then carefully trickled a handful of dirt into Stefan's grave.

They were all looking at Elena now, but she just stood there, her lips pressed firmly together, and didn't step forward. She was *angry*, Damon sensed, her rage flowing through the bond that connected them.

Finally she raised her head and stared back at her friends. "No," she said sharply. "No, I won't say good-bye.

I *do not accept this.*" She was breathing hard, and Damon felt something flutter wildly through their bond. Elena was grieving and angry and in pain, but most of all, she was terrified, frightened of losing Stefan forever. Instinctively Damon stepped forward to wrap his arms around her, cradling her safely against his chest. Her heart was beating as fast as a bird's.

"You don't have to say good-bye, princess," he said. "Not if you don't want to. But you should tell him you love him."

Elena nodded. "Of course I do," she said dully. "He knows that." She pulled away from Damon, turning her back on the open grave, and walked down toward the river.

Damon looked to Alaric, Zander, and Matt. "Finish it," he said. "She's done." Obediently, they picked up their shovels and began to fill in the grave. The first shovelful of earth hit the cloth around Stefan's body with a dry, slithering sound that made Damon wince.

He followed Elena to the riverbank and stood next to her. She was staring silently down into the water, her jaw clenched tight, her hands curled into fists. Meredith, Bonnie, and Matt joined them. Bonnie linked her arm through Elena's, and Meredith laid one hand on her shoulder, and Elena seemed to take some comfort in this.

Together, they listened to the river rushing past. After a while Bonnie said, in the puzzled voice of a hurt child, "I just don't understand what happened."

"Jack was a vampire," Elena told her, her voice dull. "Why didn't I know?"

"We should have—" Meredith began, but Damon cut her off.

"Jack was some new kind, made in a *lab*." He felt his lip curl in distaste. "He didn't have all the weaknesses our kind have." He quickly explained what had happened— the business card, the lab, the research log. "He can disguise his aura, Elena. There's no way you could have identified him. The vampires who hunted me and Katherine across Europe—he created them. He thinks he's perfected the species, made the ultimate warriors. And now he wants to get rid of the all the existing vampires. Even Stefan."

Elena made a small, hurt sound. They were all looking at Damon now, their eyes wide, and he knew what they were thinking.

Damon was next.

#TVD11Goodbye

he white lights were blinding. Meredith squinted against them and tried to struggle, but she couldn't move.

Just the dream, she told herself. *Just the same dream.* Things felt even more real this time: the lights brighter, the room less blurry around her. Her mouth was parched and sore. There was a sharp antiseptic smell in the air. She felt dizzy and nauseous.

It's only a dream, she reassured herself. *I can get through this, and then I'll wake up safe in my own bed.*

The shadowy figure moved at the edge of her vision, coming closer, and this time Meredith could see it more clearly than she ever had before. Gloved hands moving over her abdomen. A doctor in scrubs, looking down at her, face mask concealing his identity. She couldn't feel the hands moving, but she could see them. She was so numb, as if under a local anesthetic.

Carefully, the figure drew a vial of fluid into a needle, his surgical-gloved hands moving with calm precision. Meredith couldn't feel it as the needle slid into her arm, couldn't move away as the doctor pressed the plunger and the fluid slid into her veins. She arched her neck, shoving her head back against the table, flinching away as far as she could.

Although she couldn't feel the needle, the injection spread like fire across her body, her veins burning. A small, hurt gasp burst from her lips, and she tried again to get away. But she was trapped in place.

Wake up, wake up, she thought frantically.

The figure slid his mask away from his face—and beneath was Jack, his mouth quirking into a smile. Meredith whimpered, trying to push back into the table below her.

"Meredith," he said, running his hand across his face. "I thought that we should talk."

"This is a dream," Meredith said defiantly, but her voice sounded small and scared.

Jack gave a short huff of laughter. "It isn't a dream." He reached, affectionately, to brush a loose hair away from her face. "When you told me you drank vervain tea every night, I knew how to get to you. I substituted a combination of the medications I've developed and a strong sedative for your tea. It made it easy to take you for treatments.

I brought you here, and then I knocked you out again to take you home."

"What?" Meredith asked. She was having trouble drawing breath; she was panting with fear. "What treatments? Why?"

"I'm making you like me. You're perfect," Jack told her, and Meredith shuddered, sickened. "Hunters are the best recruits, and you're one hell of a hunter, Meredith. Smart and quick. Strong-willed, not like Trinity, who was so easy for that Old One to compel. You'll make an amazing vampire. When I found out your brother had been a vampire, heard rumors about you almost being changed, well." He shrugged and smiled at her, that lovely warm smile. "It seemed like it was meant to be. Together, we'll be unstoppable."

"No," Meredith said, blinking back hot tears. "I'm not like you. I don't want to be a vampire."

Jack chuckled affectionately, his hand heavy on the crown of her head. "It's not really your decision," he said. "The transformation is almost complete."

#TVD11RealityBites

* * *

"Do you think he's really gone?" Elena asked, not looking at Damon. "I mean, I came back, and so did you."

"I don't know, Elena." Damon sighed. "You came back because you weren't supposed to die, because your time hadn't passed yet. And I never should have come back. I just got lucky."

They were together on the apartment's balcony, where Stefan had liked to go to think and keep watch. The late summer smell of roses was too heavy, sickly sweet and oppressive. Elena's eyes were sore, and she rubbed at them. She was so tired of crying.

Damon lounged against the rail beside her, seeming perfectly relaxed. He had the gift of being completely still when he wanted to, without twitching and shuffling his feet like most people seemed to. It was restful to be around him, she thought. He was watching her closely, his black eyes hooded, and Elena couldn't tell what he was thinking.

"When Stefan and I were children, a long time ago," Damon said suddenly, "he was so serious. Unlike me, he tried to do the right thing. He was my father's good boy, and I hated him for it. He'd cover for me, though, try to protect me from my father and the punishments I always deserved." He grimaced, a small twitch of his lips. "Stefan would get a beating for lying to protect me. I never even thanked him."

"You were children," she said gently.

"Protecting me always got Stefan hurt," Damon went on, as if he hadn't heard her. "We fought and we were apart for centuries. Without him, I lost myself."

Elena took his hand. He felt so cold, and she rubbed her hands against his to warm it. "I was lost, too," she said. "After my parents died, I didn't really care about anything. I wanted to be the queen of the school, but it was just pride keeping me going. Stefan . . . Stefan was the first person to really *see* me, to find who I was under what I wanted everyone to see." She felt herself tearing up again, and she pressed her face against her and Damon's clasped hands, so that he wouldn't see her cry. "I'm worried I'm going to get lost again."

"I'm not going to leave you this time," Damon told her. "If nothing else, I can look after you for Stefan." His lips twisted in a wry little grin. "Not that you really need looking after."

"We can look after each other," Elena said. She was glad he was staying; there was a comfort in Damon's presence, although it didn't fill up the void that seemed to be growing inside her. Without Stefan, she felt so alone, one floating speck in a dark and empty universe. But Damon was alone, too, and right now they needed each other.

"And there's another reason I need to stay," Damon said, a new sharpness in his tone. Elena looked up at him, her attention caught. "Vengeance." He gripped her hand tighter, and she squeezed back in response. "Jack? The vampires he's created? We have to make them all pay."

The dark emptiness within Elena slowly heated and began to burn. She might be lost and alone, but, if she could get revenge for Stefan's death, her life would have purpose.

"Yes," she told him, nodding. "Vengeance."

Look out for #TVD12Unspoken

About the Author

 L. J. Smith has written a number of best-selling books and series for young adults, including *The Vampire Diaries* (now a hit TV show), *The Secret Circle*, *The Forbidden Game*, *Night World*, and the New York Times #1 bestselling *Dark Visions*. She is happiest sitting by a crackling fire in a cabin in Point Reyes, California, or walking the beaches that surround that area. She loves to hear from readers and hopes they will visit her updated website at www.ljanesmith.net.